CRIP

Written by

Darryl Harvey

Based on True Events

94th Place Films
L.A., Ca 90047

EXT. UCLA CAMPUS - DAY

Westwood is bustling with students, featuring prominent
buildings and the Bruins bear statue.

I/E. ROOM 1201 OF CAMPBELL HALL - DAY

INSERT CARD: JAN. 17, 1969

A meeting is in progress, and murmurs can be heard among a
large group of predominantly Black students. Their attire
speaks volumes; they are wearing bell-bottom pants, print
tunic tops, side-pleated dresses, mock turtleneck shirts,
gaucho knit short-sleeve shirts, and dashikis.

Another group of students, black militants, are wearing
Levi's, khaki pants, button-down shirts, Tam hats, and black
leather coats.

Among them are JOHN J. HUGGINS male African-American 23, and
ALPRENTICE "BUNCHY" CARTER male African-American 26.

At the head of the room is FLOYD HAYES male African-American
22, he addresses the students.

> FLOYD
> The High Potential Program was
> created to recruit Black and
> Chicano students. UCLA relaxed the
> academic qualifications for this
> project. The students here right
> now are direct beneficiaries of
> that project. The Black Student
> Union has pushed for a Center for
> Afro-American Studies. Chancellor
> Charles Young is supportive of this
> endeavor. The Black Student Union
> and faculty are unified in our
> desire to create the center.

There is a consensus of applause from the students.

> FLOYD (CONT'D)
> However, the center is now a point
> of contention over who's going to
> control it. Maulana "Ron" Karenga
> is being stifled and opposed at
> every turn. He has backed Dr.
> Charles Thomas, who is director of
> a health center in Watts. Dr.
> Thomas has been promoted to the
> director of Afro-American studies.
> (MORE)

                         FLOYD (CONT'D)
          There are some that oppose Dr.
          Thomas as director. As President
          of the Black Student Union, I
          welcome Maulana's advice.

We hear more grumbling from some students. Bunchy leans over
to John.

                         BUNCHY
                  (whisper)
          Karenga has his own agenda, which
          is in opposition to the Panthers.

                         JOHN
          He wants a staff, office space, and
          a generous budget.

                         BUNCHY
          We can't let that happen. Either
          the US Organization is going to
          control the center or the Panthers.

Floyd still standing at the head of the room.

                         FLOYD
          This concludes today's meeting. We
          will address any issues next week.

Students are starting to drift out when HAROLD "TUWALA"
JONES, a male African-American, 19, enters the room. John
takes notice.

                         JOHN
                  (suspicious)
          Hey man, there's Tuwala. I need to
          talk to that brother.

                         BUNCHY
          That cat is here to gather
          information for the US
          Organization.

John walks up to Tuwala and confronts him.

                         JOHN
          Are you here as a student or a spy?

                         TUWALA
          What you talkin' bout man?

Bunchy walks up and stands next to John.

                    JOHN
          Have you been given Elaine Brown a
          hard time?

                    TUWALA
          I don't know who you been talkin'
          to. I don't have a problem with
          Elaine.

                    JOHN
          Stop harassing her. You understand
          me -- brother!

                    TUWALA
          Fuck you, man.

John punches Tuwala in the face, a scuffle breaks out.
Bunchy tries to break up the fight. At that point, CLAUDE
"CHUCHESSA" HUBERT, male African-American, 21, enters the
room.

Chuchessa pulls out a gun and shoots John in the back.
Bunchy tries to take cover behind a chair and Chuchessa
shoots through the chair killing Bunchy instantly.

Mortally wounded, John, who is armed. Pulls his own gun out
as he falls, emptying it on reflex.

                                        DISSOLVE TO:

EXT. RESIDENTIAL NEIGHBORHOOD - MORNING

INSERT CARD: WATTS CALIFORNIA

A Black PAPERBOY is riding his bike and tossing NEWSPAPERS.
A newspaper lands on the walkway of a home. An African-
American MAN in his 40s, wearing pajamas, a robe, and
slippers, picks up the newspaper and opens it up.

Photos of two African-American men are on the L.A. Times
front page. The headline reads *Two Black Panther students
slain in UCLA Hall.*"

EXT. FREMONT HIGH SCHOOL - CAMPUS - DAY

MUSIC CUE: "Say It Loud, I'm Black & I'm Proud" by James
Brown.

Over an aerial view of students walking about. The music
morphs into...

                                    DISSOLVE TO:

INT. FREMONT HIGH SCHOOL - MUSIC ROOM - DAY

The High School Band playing the soulful song. STUDENT #1,
STUDENT #2, and STUDENT #3 are wearing Cardinal and Gray
Marching Band JACKETS. They are in lockstep and jamming
hard.

The music TEACHER feels the rhythm as REGGIE THOMPSON, male
African-American, 17, plays his FLUTE with extreme soul. The
sound is professional and polished. Just as the band
finishes their routine, the music Teacher beams with pride.

                    TEACHER
          That sounded great. You guys
          should be proud of yourselves.

                    STUDENT #1
          Yeah, and we look good in our new
          jackets.

                    TEACHER
          You certainly do.

                    STUDENT #2
          The school emblem is nice. Fremont
          Pathfinders marching band.

                    STUDENT #3
          Our nicknames are stitched on the
          left side, cool.

Student #3 is proud, he struts around like a turkey. Reggie,
extremely bowlegged, has a very distinctive and unusual gait
walks up.

                    REGGIE
              (not amused)
          Who's idea was this?

Some of the Students notice the nickname on Reggie's jacket
and giggle.

                    STUDENT #1
          C'mon man, don't be pissed. You
          look good in your jacket.

                    STUDENT #2
          We voted to have nicknames stitched
          on the jackets -- remember?

                    REGGIE
          I wasn't here for the vote.

                    STUDENT #3
          I know we tease you about being
          bowlegged, call you cripple
          sometimes. It was either bowlegged
          or cripple. The Teacher went with
          Crip, short for cripple.

Reggie, perturb, turns to the Teacher.

                    REGGIE
          Can this be changed?

                    TEACHER
          Sorry, Reggie, I had to place the
          order. You weren't here.

                    REGGIE
             (exasperated)
          Man, I have to walk around with
          this on my jacket.

                    TEACHER
          Don't worry Reggie. It'll grow on
          you.

The camera pushes into the nickname on Reggie's jacket, CRIP.

EXT. FREMONT HIGH SCHOOL - SCHOOL HALLWAY - DAY

The BELL RINGS. Students exit their classrooms. The music
students file out with excitement as they exit the music
room.

EXT. FREMONT HIGH SCHOOL - LUNCH AREA - DAY

Students mill about. Sitting at a table are RAYMOND
WASHINGTON male African-American, 16, and CRAIG CRADDOCK male
African-American, 15.

                    RAYMOND
          Chuchessa killed John and Bunchy.

                    CRAIG CRADDOCK
          The US Organization and the Black
          Panthers had beef.

                    RAYMOND
          That don't make sense. Two pro-
          black organizations at each other's
          throats.

                    CRAIG CRADDOCK
          The paper said the killer is on the
          run.

                    RAYMOND
          That's fucked up man. We had the
          Watts riots. Now this shit.

                    CRAIG CRADDOCK
          Brothers have to get their shit
          together man.

                    RAYMOND
          Right on.

Reggie walks up.

                    REGGIE
          What's happenin'?

They give each other the black handshake.

                    RAYMOND
          That's fucked up what happened to
          Bunchy.

                    REGGIE
          Yeah, it is. Bunchy was a positive
          influence in the community.

                    RAYMOND
          I wanted to join the Black
          Panthers. They said I was too
          young. Bunchy ran the breakfast
          program. They'd fead us in the
          mornings, before school.

                    CRAIG CRADDOCK
          I remember -- least we didn't have
          to start school on an empty
          stomach.

                    REGGIE
          Bunchy was cool. He left the
          Slausons and help start the L.A.
          Chapter of the Panthers.

                    RAYMOND
          I hope they catch them cats.

                    REGGIE
     I know who's happy Bunchy is dead.

                    RAYMOND
     The cops!

                    REGGIE
     Damn right.

                    CRAIG CRADDOCK
     Cops see all black people the same
     way -- trouble makers, always
     startin' shit.

                    RAYMOND
     I'm gonna keep startin' shit. I'm
     gonna start somethin' big.
     Somethin' that's gonna bring black
     people together. -- My own gang.

Craig and Reggie look at Raymond oddly.

                    CRAIG CRADDOCK
     What about the Avenues? Monson is
     squashin' niggas.

                    RAYMOND
     I don't give a fuck!

                    REGGIE
     Man forget about all that negative
     shit. What y'all think about the
     jacket?

Raymond and Craig walk around Reggie as he postures like a
model. They inspect the jacket closely.

                    REGGIE (CONT'D)
     Sharp, huh?

                    CRAIG CRADDOCK
     It's cool.

                    RAYMOND
     Yeah, it's cool man.
          (pointing)
     But what does this mean?

                    REGGIE
     It's spose to be a nickname.

                    CRAIG CRADDOCK
     Spose to be?

                    REGGIE
All the band members have nicknames
stitched on their jackets.

                    RAYMOND
So that's your nickname? Crip?
What the fuck does that mean.

Craig laughs.

                    REGGIE
They call me cripple because of my
bowlegs. Crip is short for Cripple
-- get it?

Raymond and Craig both laugh. Reggie frowns.

                REGGIE (CONT'D)
I knew this would happen.

I/E. HOME OF VIOLET SAMUEL - DAY

A group of teens led by Craig Craddock approaches the steps.
Craig walks up to the porch and knocks on the door. DERARD
BARTON male, African American, 11, opens the door.

                    DERARD
What's happenin', Craig?

                  CRAIG CRADDOCK
Where's Raymond?

Derard turns and shouts.

                    DERARD
Raymond, Craig's at the door.

Derard turns back to look out the door. He sees the group of
teens with Craig. Derard turns back and shouts again.

                  DERARD (CONT'D)
A bunch of your homeboys out here
too.

Raymond comes to the door and chides Denard.

                    RAYMOND
What are you shouting for?

Derard just shrugs his shoulders.

INT. HOME OF VIOLET SAMUEL - KITCHEN - DAY

VIOLET SAMUEL, African American female, 40, is slaving over a
stove cooking, pauses.

                    VIOLET
               (shouts)
          Raymond, who is that at the door?

EXT. HOME OF VIOLET SAMUEL - PORCH - CONTINUOUS

With the front door open, Raymond turns around and shouts.

                    RAYMOND
          Nobody mama, just some friends.

                    DERARD
               (mocking)
          What are you shouting for?

                    RAYMOND
          You tryin' to be funny? You wanna
          get knocked out?

                    DERARD
          And mama will knock you out.

                    RAYMOND
          Go on in your room.

                    DERARD
          You mean our room.

                    RAYMOND
          Man, just go.

Derard turns and walks off, and Craig chuckles.

                    CRAIG CRADDOCK
          Your little brother is a trip.

                    RAYMOND
          Yeah, he is. So what's happenin',
          man?

                    CRAIG CRADDOCK
          I brought some of the fellas with
          me.

                    RAYMOND
          I see. What's happenin' fellas?

Raymond steps off the porch onto the front yard.

He greets JOHN "MOON" MCDANIELS, male African-American 16, PAUL "BABY ALDEN" JONES, male African-American 15, and his brother BIG ALDEN JONES, male African-American 16.

Also in tow are L.C. BUTLER, male African-American, 16, and ELVIS DEXTER, male African-American, 16. They acknowledge each other with head nods and the black handshake.

Craig walks off the porch and joins Raymond.

>   CRAIG CRADDOCK
>   Monson's brother is looking for
>   you. He wants to settle a beef.

>   BIG ALDEN
>   What you wanna do?

>   BABY ALDEN
>   We're down with you man.

FLASHBACK:

EXT. CRAIG MONSON'S BACKYARD - DAY

CRAIG MONSON, male African-American 19, is lifting weights with two friends, DONNIE BOY, male African-American 19, and RAYMOND BURNES, male African-American 19.

Raymond Washington walks up looking agitated. As Craig is bench pressing 200 lbs., Raymond looks down at him.

>   RAYMOND
>   What's the problem with me joining
>   the Avenues?

Craig presses his last rep. He sits the weights on the barbell rack. Craig calmly sits up on the bench and gives Raymond a hard look.

>   CRAIG MONSON
>   Look, man, I told you the Avenues
>   ain't for you. Now I hear you
>   startin' a gang called the Baby
>   Avenues. Are you fucken' crazy?

>   DONNIE BOY
>   Startin' a gang, get that shit out
>   yo mind.

                         RAYMOND BURNS
          Ain't but one Avenues gang young
          brotha. Don't fuck around and get
          hurt.

They exchange intense glances, and Raymond Washington walks
away with confidence.

                         DONNIE BOY
          That dude's gon' be a problem.

END OF FLASHBACK:

EXT. HOME OF VIOLET SAMUEL - CONTINUOUS

Raymond Washington, Craig, John, Baby Alden, Big Alden,
Dexter, and L.C. are still standing in the front yard.

                         RAYMOND
          Put the word out that I'll meet
          Craig's brother at Roosevelt Park.

EXT. FREMONT HIGH SCHOOL - GYM - NIGHT

The low tone of music is heard. Puffing cigarettes while
mingling with each other is... Female African-American
students wearing miniskirts, go-go boots, flared skirts, and
wide trumpet sleeves.

The male African-American students are wearing acrylic
pullovers, dacron slacks, loafers, sport coats, turtle necks.

The line slowly moves as students make their way through the
front entrance. The door ATTENDANT takes tickets as the
camera pushes through the students...

INT. FREMONT HIGH SCHOOL - GYM - NIGHT

MUSIC CUE: "Twenty-Five Miles" by Edwin Starr.

A BANNER hangs high that reads Fremont High Homecoming Dance.
Students are on the floor dancing, "The Jerk," "Mashed
Potato," "The Pony," and "The Funky Chicken."

END MUSIC CUE:

The M.C. steps to the MICROPHONE and taps it twice with his
hand.

                    M.C.
          Hello everybody. Hope y'all are
          havin' a good time. Tonight I have
          the pleasure of introducing the
          Fremont High Homecoming King and
          Queen.

Standing adjacent to the stage are Reggie and SUSAN MILLER,
African American, female, 17.

                    M.C. (CONT'D)
          And now, the students you voted
          for. Your Homecoming King and
          Queen, Reggie Washington and Susan
          Miller. Please come up.

Reggie and Susan step on the stage to a round of applause and
cheers.

                    M.C. (CONT'D)
          Not only is Reggie the Homecoming
          King. He is a member of the
          Pathfinder Marching Band.

Reggie and Susan wave their hands acknowledging the crowd.

                    M.C. (CONT'D)
          As is our tradition. The King and
          Queen will dance together.

Reggie takes Susan by the hand and leads her off the stage to
the dance floor. The crowd parts like the Red Sea.

MUSIC CUE: "Baby Baby Don't Cry" by The Miracles.

Reggie and Susan embrace closely as they slow dance, gazing
deeply into each other's eyes. The crowd surrounds them
momentarily before everyone pairs up and joins in the slow
dance.

Off in the distance staring angrily is Craig Monson. Donnie
Boy steps next to Craig.

END MUSIC CUE:

                    DONNIE BOY
          Looks like Raymond's brother is
          making time with your girl.

                    CRAIG MONSON
          I'm going to put Reggie in check.

MUSIC CUE: "It's Your Thing" by The Isley Brothers.

Teens break out into the latest dances. Reggie and Susan break out into The Funky Chicken. By the look of them, they are having a great time.

Craig's body language is tense, anger consumes his face. Donnie Boy can feel the tension coming from Craig.

>   DONNIE BOY
>   What you gonna do man?

Craig, a scowl on his face, looks at Donnie Boy. He makes his way through the crowd, walking straight toward Reggie and Susan. Donnie Boy follows closely behind.

Susan is in the midst of doing The Funky Chicken when suddenly she is grabbed by Craig.

END MUSIC CUE:

>   CRAIG MONSON
>   We need to talk!

Susan angrily snatches away from Craig.

>   SUSAN
>   What are you doing?

>   CRAIG MONSON
>   I need to talk to you.

>   SUSAN
>   Can't you see I'm dancing, having a
>   good time? That shit can wait!

Craig violently grabs Susan, and Reggie intervenes.

>   REGGIE
>   Hey man. What's your problem?

Craig turns to confront Reggie. Donnie Boy, looking, senses heighten his posture is defensive.

>   CRAIG MONSON
>   Mind your business mutha fucka. I
>   will knock yo ass out.

The two are ready to come to blows. Susan steps in between Craig and Reggie.

>   SUSAN
>   (to Craig)
>   Why you got to ruin my night?

                         DONNIE BOY
                      (to Craig)
              Let's deal with him later.

                         CRAIG MONSON
                      (to Reggie)
              I'll see you outside nigga!

Craig and Donnie Boy walk off. Susan gives Reggie a worried
look.

EXT. FREMONT HIGH SCHOOL - GYM - NIGHT

Raymond Washington, Craig Craddock, John, Baby Alden, Big
Alden, Dexter, and L.C. have shown up. They are hardly
dressed for the occasion.

Wearing Levi's, button-down shirts, biscuit shoes, waistline
leather jackets, and Ace Deuce Hats. They are about to make
their way into the dance when...

A.C. MOSES African-American male, 13, notices Raymond. A.C.
is with two teens, ROBERT, male African-American, 15, and
GERALD, male African-American, 15. A.C. shouts out...

                         A.C.
              Raymond!

From a few yards away, Raymond turns to A.C. and takes pause.
A.C. throws both hands in the air.

                         A.C. (CONT'D)
              It's me homie, A.C.

Raymond breaks out into a smile. Raymond and his boys walk
over to A.C.

                         RAYMOND
              Got damn man, you got big. What
              the hell you been eatin'?

                         A.C.
              Looks like you been driving iron.
              You gonna bust out that coat.

Just then an angry Craig Monson, followed by Donnie Boy,
storms out of the dance. The few students that are in his
way get pushed to the side.

That gets the attention of Raymond and A.C. Craig Monson is
met by KENNY CARTER African-American male, 19, and Raymond
Burns.

>   A.C. (CONT'D)
>   Hey man, that's Craig Monson. He's
>   pissed about something.

>   RAYMOND
>   Yeah, he is.

A.C. looks to be in awe of Craig Monson.

>   A.C.
>   The Avenues, let's talk to Craig
>   about joining them. That cat gets
>   big respect from everybody.

>   RAYMOND
>   I already tried.

>   A.C.
>   What did he say?

>   RAYMOND
>   No.

>   A.C.
>   What? Why?

>   RAYMOND
>   I was recruitin' cats. Claiming
>   Avenue. He found out, said ain't
>   but one leader of The Avenues.

>   A.C.
>   You shoulda checked with him first.

>   RAYMOND
>   Fuck that nigga.

Reggie and Susan step outside. Craig Monson notices them and heads straight for Reggie and Susan, with Donnie Boy, Kenny, and Raymond Burns right behind him.

>   CRAIG MONSON
>   (hyped up)
>   Aye nigga, I ain't finished with yo
>   ass.

>   REGGIE
>   Ain't nobody scared of you nigga.

>   SUSAN
>   Craig stop actin' crazy.

>   CRAIG MONSON
>   You choose this fool over me?

                    SUSAN
          You're jealous for no reason.
          We're Homecoming King and Queen.
          That's it.

Watching from a distance, Craig Craddock nudges Raymond
Washington.

                    CRAIG CRADDOCK
          That's your brother Reggie. He's
          about to get into with Monson.

                    RAYMOND
          Come on.

Raymond Washington, Craig Craddock, John, Baby Alden, Big
Alden, Elvis, and L.C. rush over to help Reggie. A.C.
hesitates, he looks at Robert and Gerald.

                    A.C.
          Come on let's go. We have to back
          up Raymond.

                    ROBERT
          That's gonna put us against the
          Avenues.

A.C. takes off running after Raymond. Gerald looks at
Robert.

                    GERALD
          Let's go.

Robert and Gerald take off after A.C.

Raymond Washington and his boys enter the fray. A few
seconds later A.C., Robert, and Gerald run up. A crowd has
gathered, and the situation is volatile. Again Susan stands
between Reggie and Craig Monson.

                    CRAIG MONSON
          You gonna keep protecting this cat.

                    SUSAN
          I don't want to see anyone get
          hurt. And I don't want you
          fightin'.

                    RAYMOND
          Hey Craig man. Be cool.

                    CRAIG MONSON
          Listen to this nigga.

Craig stares down Raymond Washington and his homeboys.

> CRAIG MONSON (CONT'D)
> These the punks you wanted me to
> let join the Avenues? None of'em
> could make the cut.

> REGGIE
> I can handle this nigga Raymond.

> SUSAN
> Reggie shut up.

Donnie Boy runs up and punches Reggie in the jaw, he's
stunned. Before Reggie can collect himself. Craig Monson
pulls out a pistol, he shoves it in Reggie's face. *Oh's* and
ah's come from the crowd.

> RAYMOND
> What's wrong with you man?

> SUSAN
> Craig put that gun away.

Craig Monson has the gun pressed up to Reggie's face.

> CRAIG MONSON
> Stay away from my woman.

Monson slowly backs away from Reggie, he puts the gun in his
waist ban. Monson grabs Susan by the hand and drags her off.

> SUSAN
> You're squeezing my hand!

> CRAIG MONSON
> Be quiet. You're my woman.

Donnie Boy, Kenny, and Raymond Burns give everyone scathing
looks. They walk off with Craig Monson.

EXT. ROOSEVELT PARK - DAY

TEDDY MONSON, male African-American, 17, VICTOR ADAMS, male
African-American, 17, FRED STACEY, male African-American, 17,
and EDDIE HAWTHORNE, male African-American, 18, are sitting
at a picnic table hanging out.

They spot Raymond Washington, John, and Big Alden off in the
distance.

> VICTOR
> We got company.

                         FRED
              Looks like Raymond. He's got a
              couple of dudes with him.

                         TEDDY
              I've been expecting him.

                         EDDIE
              Why? What's going down?

                         TEDDY
              We fixing to see...

Raymond Washington, John, and Big Alden walk directly up to
the picnic table.

                         RAYMOND
                    (to Teddy)
              I heard you been looking for me.

                         TEDDY
              That's right.

Victor, Fred, and Eddie are looking around, not sure what to
expect.

                         RAYMOND
              You got a problem with me?

                         TEDDY
              The Avenues got a problem with you.

Fists balled up, John and Big Alden are ready for whatever
comes next.

                         VICTOR
              Is this about the other night? I
              heard what happened at the dance.

Fred stands up.

                         FRED
              Y'all looking for a fight?

                         RAYMOND
              We ain't running.

                         EDDIE
              Teddy -- You wanna get down with
              this dude?

His brow furrowed, Teddy eyes Raymond up and down. Raymond
doesn't look intimidated in the least.

                    TEDDY
          Me and you, head up.

                    RAYMOND
          Let's get down then nigga.

Teddy steps away from the picnic table. He and Raymond
square up in a fighting posture. They begin fighting,
exchanging punishing blows. Raymond counterpunches, and
Teddy goes reeling backward.

                    VICTOR
          Kick his ass, Teddy.

                    JOHN
          He don't want none, Raymond.

                    BIG ALDEN
          Yeah, knock his ass out.

Teddy gathers himself he rushes Raymond with a flurry of
blows. Raymond unfazed goes on the attack like a Pitbull.
Powerful punches to Teddy's face and body.

Teddy is fading fast, he tries to muster the strength for
another attack. Teddy throws a left, then a right. Raymond
fens off the blows.

Teddy is bleeding he's breathing heavily. Sensing Teddy
doesn't have much left, Raymond finishes him. A thunderous
left hook and right cross send Teddy crashing to the ground.

Raymond standing victorious puts the Avenue gang member on
notice.

                    RAYMOND
          Shits about to change. Scores are
          being settled.

EXT. HAMBURGER STAND 81ST AND AVALON - DAY

CUSTOMERS mill about as Craig Monson, standing at the window
orders some food.

                    CRAIG MONSON
          Give me a cheeseburger, fries, and
          a Coke. -- Hold the onions.

A CAR cruises by and makes a U-turn. Behind the wheel is
RONALD JOE WASHINGTON, male African-American, 22.

Ronald pulls in the front, making an abrupt stop, and he hastily jumps out of the car. Before Craig realizes what's going on, Ronald is in his face.

> RONALD
> (upset)
> Nigga you crazy pulling a gun on my brother?

Craig backs up slightly and takes a defensive posture.

> CRAIG MONSON
> You better back up fool.

> RONALD
> Let's see how tuff you are without a gun.

> CRAIG MONSON
> Oh, it's like that.

> RONALD
> Yeah nigga, it's like that.

Ronald begins swinging furiously. Customers quickly move out of the way. Craig blocks some of the blows and counterpunches.

Ronald takes a left and right from Craig, they circle each other as if in a boxing ring. An EMPLOYEE shouts from the order window.

> EMPLOYEE
> You guys cut that out! Stop that fighting right now!

The Employee's pleas go unheard.

> CRAIG
> What's up nigga.

> RONALD
> (panting)
> You know what's up nigga. Me and you head up.

> CRAIG
> You gon' end up on yo back.

Ronald rushes Craig, and they lock up and wrestle, tumbling over a table. Several customers break them up. The hulkish Craig Monson can hardly be contained.

                    CRAIG MONSON
          C'mon, I ain't finished with yo
          ass.

Ronald is being held back by a customer.

                    RONALD
          You might scare these other cats,
          but you don't scare me, mutha
          fucka.

The Employee pokes their head out of the order window.

                    EMPLOYEE
          I'm calling the police, you hear
          me!

                    RONALD
          This shit ain't over.

Ronald hops in his car and speeds off.

INT. HOME OF VIOLET SAMUEL - LIVING ROOM - DAY

Violet is seated at the dining table eating. Derard is
sitting on the couch watching TV. The front door opens, it's
Ronald, he looks disheveled. Violet recognizes that
something is amiss.

                    VIOLET
          Ronald Joe, you, you, all right?

                    RONALD
          Yeah, mama.

                    VIOLET
          Boy, you sure you ok?

                    RONALD
          Mama -- I'm fine.

Ronald walks past Violet in a huff, and Denard, wide-eyed,
looks on.

INT. HOME OF VIOLET SAMUEL - BEDROOM - DAY

The atmosphere is serious. Reggie, Raymond, and DONALD RAY
WASHINGTON, male African-American, 20, are huddling together.

                    DONALD RAY
          You don't want the situation to get
          out of hand.

Ronald comes in, he shuts the door behind him.

                    RONALD
          Donald Ray, it already is. I had a
          fight with Big Monson.

                    REGGIE
          You look like it.

                    RONALD
          He shouldn't have pulled a gun on
          you.

                    DONALD RAY
          Now y'all at odds with the Avenues.

                    RAYMOND
          I had a fight with Monson's
          brother, Teddy.

Ronald, with his hand, looks over Raymond's face.

                    RONALD
          You don't look too bad. Busted lip
          though.

                    RAYMOND
          Yeah, but I put that dude on his
          back.

Donald gives his brothers a serious look.

                    DONALD RAY
          You guys gon' have to watch yo
          back. The Avenues ain't no joke.

                    RAYMOND
          Fuck them, I'm gon' start my own
          gang.

Derard opens the door, he meanders his way in.

                    DERARD
          What y'all rappin' bout?

                    RAYMOND
          None of yo business. Now get out
          of here.

                    DERARD
          How you gon' put me out my own
          room?

                        DONALD RAY
            Go on back in there with Mama.
            We're talkin' business.

                        DERARD
                    (serious)
            Alright, alright. If you need me,
            just let me know. I'm down for
            whatever, dig.

Derard walks out, he shuts the door behind him. Reggie,
Raymond, Ronald, and Donald look at each other, with slight
chuckles, and head-scratching.

EXT. HOME OF AUNT MINNIE - DAY

MUSIC CUE: "Hot Fun in the Summertime" by Sly & The Family
Stone.

The camera pushes through the front door.

INT. HOME OF AUNT MINNIE - LIVING ROOM - DAY

A cigarette hangs from the mouth of John "Moon" McDaniels.
He stands next to the HIFI, sorting through 45 records. Paul
Baby Alden Jones and Big Alden Jones are smoking marijuana.

                        BIG ALDEN
            Moon, you wanna hit this joint man?

Baby Alden takes a long pull from the joint. He inhales and
starts coughing.

                        BABY ALDEN
            This is some good shit man, here.

Baby Alden passes the joint to John.

                        JOHN
            I'm cool man, I'm sky-high.

Big Alden takes the joint from Baby Alden.

                        BIG ALDEN
            Let me show you how to do this
            little bro.

Big Alden takes a long drag from the joint. He inhales, then
begins coughing. John and Baby Alden laugh.

                    JOHN
          What are you trying to do? You
          gon' hurt yourself.

                    BABY ALDEN
          That's some righteous weed man.

END MUSIC CUE:

INT. HOME AUNT MINNIE - KITCHEN - CONTINUOUS

A crap game is underway. Banter and cigarette smoke are in
the air. Several DOLLAR BILLS and COINS are on the floor.
VERTIS SWAN African-American male 16, is shaking the DICE.

                    VERTIS
          My point is nine.

RAY RHONE, African-American male 16, L.C. Butler, Elvis
Dexter, SLEEPY, African-American male 15, and ECKY, African-
American male 15, look on in anticipation.

Vertis blows on the dice and throws them, they roll and land
on eight.

                    ECKY
          Bet a dollar he don't hit his
          point. Who gon' cover me?

Ecky lays a dollar on the floor. Vertis picks up the dice.

                    ELVIS
          I'll cover, bet he hit his point.

Elvis lays his dollar on the floor. Vertis is shaking the
dice.

                    VERTIS
          Come on, get yo bets down. I'm
          fixin' to roll'em.

                    SLEEPY
          Dollar he hit his point.

Sleepy tosses a dollar bill onto the floor.

                    L.C.
          Roll the dice man, come on.

                    VERTIS
          Ready to lose your money, huh?
               (shaking dice)
          Bring it home to Papa.

Vertis rolls the dice, a seven comes up.

                    VERTIS (CONT'D)
          Damn.

                    L.C.
          You lose. I'm on the dice now.

L.C. picks up his dollar.

                    ECKY
          Elvis, Sleepy, he didn't hit his
          point. Thanks for the bread.

Ecky picks up his money. Raymond Washington walks in, he
gestures to Ray Rhone. The guys are caught up in the crap
game. Ray Rhone walks up to Raymond.

                    RAYMOND
          Come on.

                    RAY RHONE
          Where we going?

                    RAYMOND
          Just follow me.

They walk down the hallway and stop at a bedroom door.
Raymond turns to Ray Rhone.

                    RAYMOND (CONT'D)
          You want some pussy?

                    RAY RHONE
          Do I want some pussy?

                    RAYMOND
          Yeah nigga, do you want some pussy.

                    RAYMOND (CONT'D)
          Hell yeah. Hell yeah, I want some
          pussy.

INT. HOME OF AUNT MINNIE - LIVING ROOM - CONTINUOUS

John is passed out on the couch. Baby Alden, standing next
to the HIFI, sorts through 45 records. Big Alden, is rolling
a marijuana cigarette and licks the zig zap paper.

                    BIG ALDEN
          What you gon' play?

                    BABY ALDEN
          I think I'm gon' play this.

Baby Alden sits a 45 record on the phonograph, and the needle
drops. We hear the crackling of the record.

MUSIC CUE: "The Nitty Gritty" by Gladys Knight & The Pips.

Baby Alden bobs his head to the groove.

INT. HOME OF AUNT MINNIE - BEDROOM - CONTINUOUS

The door opens Raymond enters followed by Ray Rhone shutting
the door behind him.

END MUSIC CUE:

In the bed, Craig Craddock is kissing a gorgeous teen, HELEN
African American female 15. She is scantily clad and
obviously high.

                    HELEN
               (smiling)
          Raymond, you brought a friend.
          Here, you want one?

Helen extends her arm and opens her hand. In the palm of her
hand are several PILLS.

                    RAY RHONE
          What's that?

                    HELEN
          Red Devils, take one.

                    RAY RHONE
          No thanks.

                    HELEN
          What about you Raymond -- Want one?

                    RAYMOND
          Nah, I'm cool.

                    HELEN
          Aw, you guys are no fun. You have
          to be high if we gon' get down.

Craig takes a pill from Helen's hand. He pops it in his
mouth and chases it with a swig of beer.

                         CRAIG
          You heard her man. Gots to be high
          if we gon' get down. And I want to
          get down.

Craig takes his shirt off and unbuckles his trousers. He
starts to fondle Helen. In a euphoric state, Helen just
giggles and laughs.

                         RAY RHONE
                    (to Raymond)
          I'm cool man. You and Craig can
          have her.

Ray Rhone leaves shutting the door behind him.

INT. HOME OF AUNT MINNIE - LIVING ROOM - CONTINUOUS

Ray Rhone enters and looks around. Snoring, John is still
sleeping on the couch. Big Alden and Baby Alden are gone.

INT. HOME OF AUNT MINNIE - KITCHEN - CONTINUOUS

Ray Rhone walks into the chatter of L.C., Elvis, Vertis,
Sleepy, and Ecky who are still gambling.

INT. HOME OF AUNT MINNIE - LIVING ROOM - CONTINUOUS

Just then, the front door opens. Aunt MINNIE SIMS walks in,
a female African-American in her 40s. To her dismay, she
sees John snoring on the couch.

                         AUNT MINNIE
          What the hell?

Aunt Minnie hears L.C.'s voice coming from the kitchen.

                         L.C. (O.S.)
          Eleven! Give me my money.

Aunt Minnie walks by John as he snores and adjusts his
sleeping position.

INT. HOME OF AUNT MINNIE - KITCHEN - CONTINUOUS

At the entrance, Aunt Minnie looks astonished, with a glare
in her eyes.

> AUNT MINNIE
> (yells)
> Get yo asses out ma house now. I'm
> calling the po-lice.

INT. HOME OF AUNT MINNIE - LIVING ROOM - CONTINUOUS

The yell wakes John out of his sleep, he yarns and stretches.

INT. HOME OF AUNT MINNIE - KITCHEN - CONTINUOUS

Ray Rhone, L.C., Elvis, Vertis, Ecky, and, Sleepy runs past
Aunt Minnie almost knocking her down.

INT. HOME OF AUNT MINNIE - LIVING ROOM - CONTINUOUS

John awake on the couch looks confused.   Ray Rhone, L.C.,
Elvis, Sleepy, and Vertis race past him.

Ecky, running, grabs John.

> ECKY
> (excitedly)
> C'mon nigga, let's get outta here.

EXT. HOME OF AUNT MINNIE - CONTINUOUS

The front door burst open. Ray Rhone, L.C., Elvis, Vertis,
Ecky, Sleepy, Ecky, and John race off in different
directions.

INT. HOME OF AUNT MINNIE - KITCHEN - CONTINUOUS

Aunt Minnie, fuming, stands there.

> AUNT MINNIE
> (low tone)
> Helen.
> (yells)
> Helen!!!!!

INT. HOME OF AUNT MINNIE - BEDROOM - DAY

Helen, high, is lying in bed naked.

> HELEN
> (giggling)
> Sounds like my Aunt Minnie is here.

Raymond and Craig are hurriedly getting dressed. Craig, still under the influence of drugs, is unsteady as he pulls his pants up. Raymond looks around with uncertainty.

> RAYMOND
> Get it together man.

The door swings open. Standing there, looming, Aunt Minnie has a shocked look on her face.

> AUNT MINNIE
> Helen. What's going on here?

Helen pulls the bedsheet over her.

> HELEN
> They raped me.

> RAYMOND
> That's a lie.

> CRAIG
> (mumbling)
> Ah, ah... Nah... It ain't like that.

Standing, Aunt Minnie, fury in her eyes.

> AUNT MINNIE
> Out, out, out.

Raymond slithers by an angry Aunt Minnie. Craig scurries by, stumbles, and falls. Raymond quickly helps Craig to his feet. The two rush off.

I/E. POLICE SQUAD CAR - STREET - EVENING

A DISPATCHER broadcast comes over the radio. OFFICER #1 and OFFICER #2, both white males, listen intently.

> DISPATCHER (V.O.)
> All units be on the lookout for two
> black male teens. Reported two
> sixty-one in the area of Florence
> and Central. Suspects fled the
> scene on foot.

OFFICER #1, driving north on Avalon Blvd, makes an abrupt U-turn and accelerates at high speed.

EXT. SOUTH LOS ANGELES RESIDENTIAL NEIGHBORHOOD - EVENING

Raymond Washington is strolling when an LAPD squad car slowly
cruises up the street. The squad car pulls alongside Raymond
as he's walking. Officer #2 points the mounted LIGHT on the
squad car and shines it on Raymond.

                    OFFICER #2
          Hey, you hold it right there.

Raymond stops, light shining on his face. He holds a hand up
to shield his eyes.

                    RAYMOND
          Damn.

Officer #2 and Officer #1 quickly exit the squad car. Both
Officers aggressively grab Raymond and slam him onto the hood
of the squad car. Officer #1 pats Raymond down.

                    OFFICER #2
          Where are you going?

                    RAYMOND
          On my way home.

                    OFFICER #2
          Where are you coming from?

                    RAYMOND
          A friend's house.

                    OFFICER #1
          He's clean. No I.D.

                    OFFICER #2
          What's your name?

                    RAYMOND
          Raymond.

                    OFFICER #2
          What's your last name?

                    RAYMOND
          Washington.

Officer #2 jesters to Officer #1.

                    OFFICER #2
          Run a check on him.

Officer #1 walks around the squad car, and opens the door.
He can be seen speaking into the car radio mic.

                    OFFICER #2 (CONT'D)
          How old are you?

                         RAYMOND
          Sixteen.

                         OFFICER #2
          You're pretty big for your age.
          Look, if the check comes back
          clean. You're free to go.

Officer #1 walks up.

                         OFFICER #1
          He has a juvie arrest record. He
          also fits the description of the
          two sixty-one.

                         OFFICER #2
          I'm going to have to take you in
          for questioning.

Raymond, dejection washes over him. Officer #2 turns Raymond
around and handcuffs him.

INT. HOME OF VIOLET SAMUEL - EVENING

Reggie and Derard are sitting at the dinner table doing
homework. Violet is sitting on the couch watching TV when
the phone RINGS.

                         DERARD
          I'll get it.

Derard races to answer the phone.

                         REGGIE
          Why are you rushin' to the phone?
          Ain't nobody calling you.

Derard picks up the receiver, then covers it with his hand.

                         DERARD
          It might be my homeboy -- Hello.

Raymond's subdued voice can be heard on the phone.

                         RAYMOND (V.O.)
          Derard, let me speak to Mama.

                         DENARD
          Mama, it's Raymond.

Reggie looks up curiously from doing his homework. Violet takes the phone from Denard.

                    VIOLET
          Hey.

                    RAYMOND (V.O.)
          Mama, I been arrested.

                    VIOLET
          Arrested, for what?

                    RAYMOND (V.O.)
          They trying to charge me with rape.

                    VIOLET
          Rape! Boy, can't you stay out of
          trouble?

INT. CRAIG CRADDOCKS HOUSE - BEDROOM - NIGHT

Craig is lying on his bed, he appears to be asleep when the phone RINGS. Craig drags himself to the phone, he picks up the receiver.

                    CRAIG
               (groggy)
          Hello.

Reggie is on the other end, he sounds alarmed.

                    REGGIE (V.O.)
          Craig, Raymond's been arrested.

                    CRAIG
          Bullshit.

                    REGGIE (V.O.)
          He just called the house, told my
          mama he's been arrested for rape.

                    CRAIG
          Fuck.

INT. LOS ANGELES POLICE STATION - NIGHT

Violet is at the front desk talking to a white male POLICE OFFICER, she is visibly upset.

                    VIOLET
          I need some answers.

                    POLICE OFFICER
          Ma'am, I suggest you go home. Wait
          for your son to call you.

                    VIOLET
          My son is sixteen years old. He
          doesn't have an attorney, his
          rights are being violated.

Just then Craig walks up.

                    CRAIG
          Raymond ain't rape nobody.

                    VIOLET
          Craig -- Boy what are you doing
          here?

                    CRAIG
          Raymond is innocent.

                    POLICE OFFICER
          What's your name?

                    CRAIG
          Craig Craddock.

                    POLICE OFFICER
          Oh yeah, you're one of the suspects
          we're looking for.

The Police Officer gestures to a uniformed cop, BILL, a white
male 40, who walks over.

                    POLICE OFFICER (CONT'D)
          Aye Bill, detain this kid. He's a
          suspect wanted in the two sixty-
          one.

Bill immediately handcuffs Craig.

                    VIOLET
          Craig, you mixed up in this too?

As Bill ushers Craig off.

                    CRAIG
          This is a mistake, Miss Samuel.

                    BILL
          C'mon, let's go.

INT. HOME OF AUNT MINNIE - LIVING ROOM - DAY

Helen is crying as DETECTIVE #1 white male, and DETECTIVE #2
white male questions her. Aunt Minnie looks very concerned.

                    DETECTIVE #1
          Adriamycin was found in your room.
          You were under the influence when
          the police arrived.

                    AUNT MINNIE
          What is Adriamycin?

                    DETECTIVE #2
          A popular drug among teens. The
          street name is Red Devil.

                    AUNT MINNIE
          My God! Helen, where did the drugs
          come from?

                    DETECTIVE #1
          Well, Helen. You heard your Aunt.

                    HELEN
          I don't know. I don't know.

                    DETECTIVE #2
          Did those boys force themselves on
          you? Or did you let them?

                    AUNT MINNIE
          Of course, they forced her.

                    DETECTIVE #2
          Miss Sims, please.

                    DETECTIVE #1
          Now, Helen, your Aunt reported that
          you were raped. We need to hear
          that from you.

                    HELEN
          I can't remember. I just can't
          remember.

Helen breaks down crying. The detectives are clearly
frustrated.

EXT. HOME OF AUNT MINNIE - DAY

DETECTIVE #1 and DETECTIVE #2 exit the front door. They walk
over to an unmarked police car.

                    DETECTIVE #1
          The charges won't stick. Not
          without her cooperation.

                    DETECTIVE #2
          Yeah. Just a bunch of teens
          smoking weed and popping pills.

EXT. FREMONT HIGH SCHOOL - DAY

It's lunchtime, students are milling about. We see the usual
suspects, Raymond, Elvis, Vertis, John, and Reggie hanging
out on the quad. Some of the students murmur and stare at
Raymond.

                    VERTIS
          Man, that lady was pissed.

                    ELVIS
          We could of all been locked up.

                    REGGIE
               (to Raymond)
          You lucky the rape charges were
          dropped.

                    RAYMOND
          We didn't rape her.

                    JOHN
          I'm glad I left.

                    RAYMOND
          Aw, Moon, you scared of pussy.

All the guys laugh except John and Reggie. PEE WEE, an
African American female, 16, walks up, and she confronts
Raymond.

                    PEE WEE
               (angry)
          Did you rape that girl?

                    RAYMOND
          What girl?

                    PEE WEE
          It's all over school. Everybody is
          talkin' bout it.

                    RAYMOND
          I don't care what you heard. I
          ain't rape nobody.

Holding school books, Helen walks up.

> HELEN
> Hi Raymond. I'm sorry you got
> arrested. I didn't snitch.

Raymond looks at Helen with a scowl. Helen with a sheepish
look, can tell by Raymond's facial expression to keep quiet.

> PEE WEE
> I heard you let niggas run a train
> on you?

> HELEN
> Ain't nobody run a train on me.
> That's bullshit.

Pee Wee gets in Helen's face.

> PEE WEE
> Then what happened?

Raymond gets in between them.

> HELEN
> Nothing happened. Just a
> misunderstanding.

> PEE WEE
> Hoe.

> HELEN
> Raymond, you need to do something
> about her.

Helen walks off.

> RAYMOND
> Pee Wee you trippin'.

> PEE WEE
> I will beat that bitch ass.

> RAYMOND
> Look, you're my girl. Stop
> worrying about some other broad.

INT. HOME OF VIOLET SAMUEL - BEDROOM - EVENING

Raymond Washington and Craig Craddock are hanging out.

                    CRAIG
          Man, I thought we were going to
          prison.

                    RAYMOND
          Nah, they would've put us in juvie
          or camp.

                    CRAIG
          So what we gon' do about the
          Avenues? Monson ain't gone lay
          down.

                    RAYMOND
          All of us have to stick together.

The door opens, Derard walks in.

                    RAYMOND (CONT'D)
          What are you doing here?

                    DERARD
          This is my room too. If you put me
          out, I'm gon' tell mama.

Raymond looks angry.

                    RAYMOND
          Alright. Sit over there and be
          cool.

Derard, smiling --

                    DERARD
          Ok, ok. I'll be cool man.

Craig chuckles.

                    CRAIG
          Your brother is a trip.

                    RAYMOND
          I need to come up with a name for
          us. A name that will make people
          take notice.

                    CRAIG
          Well, the baby Avenues is out.

                    RAYMOND
          I want our gang to be like the
          Panthers. Stand for something.

                    CRAIG
          I can dig it, man.

                    RAYMOND
          When our gang steps on the scene,
          we get complete respect.

                    CRAIG
          Right on brotha!

Craig gives Raymond five. Derard is fixated on the two, he
listens intently.

                    CRAIG (CONT'D)
          So what should we call the gang?

                    RAYMOND
          What about the Wildcats?

                    CRAIG
          That's the name of a basketball
          team.

                    RAYMOND
          The Knights, that's it.

                    CRAIG
          Hell nah.

                    RAYMOND
          The Mascots.

                    CRAIG
          Mascots, for real. Who gon'
          respect a Mascot?

Pondering, Raymond paces back and forth. Looking down at the
floor, he notices a SNEAKER with a word written on the side
of it.

                    RAYMOND
          Derard, hand me that shoe.

Derard picks up the sneaker, he hands it to Raymond.

                    DERARD
          You know Reggie don't like you
          wearing his stuff. You already got
          his shirt on.

                    RAYMOND
          Shut yo ass up.

Raymond looks at the word CRIP written on the side of the
sneaker. He hands the sneaker to Craig.

>   CRAIG
>   What? It's just your brother's
>   tennis shoe.

>   RAYMOND
>   You see what he wrote on the shoe?

>   CRAIG
>   Crip? That's the nickname the band
>   gave him -- So what.

>   RAYMOND
>   That's what I'm calling the gang.

>   CRAIG
>   Crip, that don't mean nothing.

>   RAYMOND
>   (gazing)
>   Crip -- I'm gon' make it mean
>   something.

EXT. FREMONT HIGH SCHOOL FOOTBALL FIELD - BLEACHERS - DAY

Raymond Washington, Craig Craddock, John Moon McDaniels, Paul
Baby Alden Jones, Big Alden Jones, L.C. Butler, Elvis Dexter,
Vertis Swan, Sleepy, and Ecky are huddled together.

>   RAYMOND
>   I wanted a name that would separate
>   us from the rest of the other
>   gangs. The Avenues, The Slausons,
>   The Businessmen, The Walnuts, The
>   Gladiators.

>   CRAIG
>   We're young. The other gangs,
>   their older dudes. They see us as
>   kids.

>   ECKY
>   The older cats think they can just
>   kick our ass, and run us off.

>   RAYMOND
>   That shit changes as of today.

>   SLEEPY
>   So what's the name you came up
>   with?

                    RAYMOND
Crip.

                    SLEEPY
        (puzzled)
Crip?

                    CRAIG
That's the same thing I said.

                    ELVIS
What does it stand for?

                    RAYMOND
We gon' make it stand for
something. I want us to be like
the Black Panthers -- Soldiers.
Protect our neighborhood. Don't
take no shit from nobody -- Another
gang, the cops, the man, whoever.

                    VERTIS
How are cats gon' know who we are?

                    L.C.
We just look like a group of guys
hanging out.

                    RAYMOND
I want us to dress like the
Panthers. Not only did they look
cool, they looked tuff. Button-
down dress shirts, Khakis, biscuit
shoes, leather coats, the hats.

                    BABY ALDEN
You definitely knew a Black Panther
when you saw one.

                    BIG ALDEN
Those cats had style.

                    RAYMOND
That's what I'm talkin' bout --
style. It shows we mean business.

                    JOHN
So what's the rules? Can anybody
be a Crip?

                    RAYMOND
No cowards allowed, cats that want
to join have to prove they are down
with what a Crip is about.
                    (MORE)

                    RAYMOND (CONT'D)
          No guns, accept a challenge from a
          rival gang. A rat will suffer the
          consequences. A trader will be
          punished and kicked out the gang.
          We have to kick ass and put all
          other gangs on notice. Either
          you're a Crip or you get run over.

EXT. SAVOY SKATING RINK 78TH AND CENTRAL - NIGHT

MUSIC CUE: "Runaway Child, Running Wild" by The Temptations.

A line of teenagers with skates in hand, and some slung over
their shoulders anxiously wait to enter. At the entrance
patrons eagerly pay ¢70 to get in.

INT. SAVOY SKATING RINK 78TH AND CENTRAL - NIGHT

Teenagers on skates circle the wooden rink, dancing to their
own versions of the cha-cha and the Slauson shuffle. Their
arms move, their feet glide, and their bodies sway.

Skating close together, some of the teens link arms, kick
their knees high, and crisscross their legs while still
bopping to the beat.

END MUSIC CUE:

Stepping out of the crowd into the spotlight, the Crips are
on the scene. Raymond surveys the crowd. With him are Craig
Craddock, John Moon McDaniels, Paul Baby Alden Jones, Big
Alden Jones, and L.C. Butler.

They walk with a certain style, a gangsta lean. A type of
limp in their strut that makes it seem cool to walk that way.

Even their skating style on the rink, as displayed by Elvis,
Vertis, Sleepy, and Ecky -- they look cool.

                    CRAIG
                 (to Raymond)
          Check them cats out.

Raymond takes a long, hard stare. Several black male teens
are sporting club JACKETS with a prominent insignia on the
back that says CARAVANS. They appear to be arrogant and
disrespectful, even tripping one of the SKATERS.

                    RAYMOND
          We gon' have to let them know
          what's happenin'.

Raymond walks over in the direction of the Caravans group.
He's followed by Craig, John, Big Alden, Baby Alden, and L.C.
Looking very serious, Raymond confronts the Caravans.

                    RAYMOND (CONT'D)
          What you cats spose to be, a gang?

The Caravans look at each other oddly. A member of their
group steps up to Raymond. This is CARAVANS #1.

                    CARAVANS #1
          We're a club nigga. What's it to
          you?

                    RAYMOND
          I don't like the way y'all acting
          in here.

                    CARAVANS #1
          What are you security or something?

Some of the Caravans members laugh.

                    RAYMOND
          This is Crip nigga.

                    CARAVANS #1
          Crip? What the fuck is that?

                    RAYMOND
          You fixing to find out.

Standing a few feet away watching, sensing trouble, is a big
burly black man. This is the MANAGER, he quickly intervenes.

                    MANAGER
          What's going on here? You guys
          looking to start some shit. This
          ain't the place.

                    CARAVANS #1
          Everything is cool.

                    RAYMOND
          We'll catch you niggas outside.

                    CARAVANS #1
          We ain't going nowhere.

EXT. SAVOY SKATING RINK 78TH AND CENTRAL - NIGHT

Out front, the crowd is exiting along with members of the
Caravans group. Waiting for them is Raymond, Craig, John,
Baby Alden, Big Alden, L.C., Elvis, Vertis, Sleepy, and Ecky.

                    RAYMOND
          Aye, nigga what's up.

The Caravans take notice. They hastily make their way over
to Raymond and his boys.

                    CARAVANS #1
          You want some of this fool?

                    RAYMOND
          You don't come into Crip
          neighborhood startin' shit.

                    CARAVANS #1
          Fuck you and this neighborhood.

Raymond punches Caravans #1 in the face. It's an all-out
melee between the Crip gang and the Caravans. Raymond is
pummeling Caravans #1, the fighting is fierce.

A Caravans member pulls out a switchblade on Craig, this is
Caravans #2. He lunges at Craig, missing him by inches.
Ecky comes out of nowhere, he punches Caravans #2.

Ecky and Caravans #2 struggle over the switchblade. The two
hit the ground hard. Ecky get's up, switchblade in hand, and
he looks down. Caravans #2 is lying on the ground in a fetal
position, trembling.

                    ECKY
               (shouts)
          Let's get out of here.

EXT. FOSTERS FREEZE - NIGHT

Roller Skates sit on tabletops. Teens are ordering food,
others are sitting around eating burgers. Amongst them,
seated at table benches are Raymond, Craig, Ecky, Vertis,
John, Big Alden, Baby Alden, Sleepy, Elvis, and L.C.

                    VERTIS
          We kicked those cats' asses, man.

Vertis slaps five with Raymond.

                    RAYMOND
          They came looking for static. I
          had to fire on that chump. The
          Caravans -- fuck them.

Several LAPD SQUAD CARS pulls up. White male officers
wearing hard hats quickly exit the squad cars. Wheeling
NIGHTSTICKS, they roust Raymond and his gang.

                    RAYMOND (CONT'D)
          Hey, man what's happenin'?

In a threatening manner, OFFICER #3 pounds a nightstick in
his hand.

                    OFFICER #3
          Alright, over there. Move your
          asses.

The officers corral the gang and line them up parallel on the
sidewalk.

                    OFFICER #3 (CONT'D)
          Search them for weapons.

                    CRAIG
          Man, this shit ain't cool.

Officer #3 walks up to Craig.

                    OFFICER #3
          Oh, yeah.

Officer #3 shoves his nightstick into Craig's stomach. Craig
grimaces and drops to his knees. Raymond steps forward.

                    RAYMOND
          That's bullshit man!

Two Officers immediately restrain Raymond. Officer #3 get's
in Raymond's face nightstick at the ready.

                    OFFICER #3
          You want the same treatment black
          boy?

Silent, Raymond gives Officer #3 a hard look. The officers
aggressively shakedown Vertis, L.C., Elvis, Big Alden, Baby
Alden, Sleepy, Ecky, and John. OFFICER #4 with excessive
force searches Big Alden.

                    BIG ALDEN
          C'mon, man got damn!

That response prompts Officer #4 to swiftly slam Big Alden to
the pavement. MURMURS can be heard from the crowd of teens.
A black male, TEEN #1 appalled, lashes out.

                    TEEN #1
          Aye man, you don't have to treat
          him like that.

Officer #4, knee in Big Alden's back.

                    OFFICER #4
          You want to join him?

                    RAYMOND
          This shit ain't right man!

                    OFFICER #3
          Ain't right. I'll show your black
          ass what's right.

Officer #3 forcefully grabs Raymond hustles him to the squad
car, then slams him face down on the hood. Officer #3
handcuffs Raymond.

                    RAYMOND
          What the hell you doin'?

                    OFFICER #3
          You're under arrest.

                    RAYMOND
          For what?

                    OFFICER #3
          Disturbing the peace and resisting
          arrest.

Officer #3 puts Raymond in the back of the squad car.
Officer #4 walks up.

                    OFFICER #4
          They're all clean.

Officer #3 walks up to the crowd of teens.

                    OFFICER #3
          These kids here are hoodlums, there
          bad news. I suggest you stay away
          from them.

He then turns to Craig, Vertis, L.C., Elvis, Big Alden, Baby
Alden, Sleepy, Ecky, and John.

                    OFFICER #3 (CONT'D)
          I'm letting you off with a warning.
          Whatever you call yourselves.
          Whatever kind of gang you think you
          are, we're watching.

Officer #3 and the other officers get in their squad cars and
drive off.

INT. HOME OF VIOLET SAMUEL - LIVING ROOM - NIGHT

L.V. BARTON, a male African American, in his 40s, sits at the
dining table with Violet.

                    L.V. BARTON
          How are the boys?

                    VIOLET
          Ronald Joe has been drafted.

                    L.V. BARTON
          Wow, Vietnam. Damn.

                    VIOLET
          Donald Ray has been putting in
          applications, he's trying to find a
          permanent job. Reggie is doing
          well in school, he has his music to
          focus on.

                    L.V. BARTON
          You think he'll go anywhere with
          it?

                    VIOLET
          Who knows.

                    L.V. BARTON
          What about Raymond?

                    VIOLET
          I don't know what I'm gonna do with
          that boy. The police arrested him
          recently, fortunately, the charges
          were dropped.

                    L.V. BARTON
          Violet, you keep praying.
          Hopefully, things will work out.

                    VIOLET
               (deep breath)
          Yeah...
                    (MORE)

                        VIOLET (CONT'D)
                    (raise voice)
              Derard, get out here. Your
              father's waiting.

                        DENARD (O.S.)
              OK, I'm coming.

Derard walks in with a suitcase.

                        DERARD
              I had to pack a few things.

                        VIOLET
              Boy, you not going out of town.
              You're just staying the weekend
              with your father.

                        L.V. BARTON
              Sorry, I'm so late. Working that
              swing shift, I don't get off till
              ten.

                        DERARD
              That's OK Dad.

Derard kisses Violet on the cheek, and L.V. gives her a hug.

                        L.V. BARTON
              I'll see you in a few days.

                        DERARD
              Bye, Mama.

                        VIOLET
              Bye -- You behave yourself.

                        DERARD
              I will.

L.V. and Derard exit the front door. No sooner than Violet
shuts the front door the phone RINGS. Violet walks over to
the lampstand she picks up the phone.

                        VIOLET
              Hello.

Violet's body language displays a wide range of emotions that
hit her all at once, anger, disgust, and sadness.

INT. LOS ANGELES COUNTY PROBATION DEPARTMENT - DAY

INSERT CARD: THREE WEEKS LATER

Sitting behind his desk is PHIL FOSTER white male, in his 30s. In front of him sits Raymond and Violet.

                    PHIL
          Miss Samuel, I'm Phil Foster. I've
          been assigned to your son's case.
          I'm his probation officer. He'll
          be reporting to me once a month.

                    VIOLET
          You hear that Raymond.

                    RAYMOND
          Yeah, Mama.

                    PHIL
          Raymond, you missed about a month
          of school. It's up to you if you
          want to get back on track.

Raymond slouched in the chair, his demeanor is dismissive.

                    VIOLET
          Are you listening to the man
          Raymond?

                    RAYMOND
          I'm listening Mama.

                    PHIL
          It starts with your attitude. You
          keep running into the police. This
          gang your hanging with -- that's
          nothing but trouble.

                    VIOLET
          Mr. Foster, what happens if he
          violates probation?

                    PHIL
          He could do a year in Los Padrinos
          Juvenile Hall. The judge went easy
          on him. He put Raymond on
          probation for one year.

EXT. LOS ANGELES COUNTY PROBATION DEPARTMENT - DAY

The front door opens. Raymond walks out followed by Violet, she is livid.

                    VIOLET
          Boy, you better get yourself
          together and do it fast.

                    RAYMOND
          Mama, the police are racist. Black
          people are a targets.

                    VIOLET
          I don't wanna hear that shit.
          You're involved with gangs. You're
          making it easy for the police to
          throw you in jail, or kill you.
          It's as simple as that. And if the
          police don't kill you, damn it
          gangs will!

EXT. FREMONT HIGH SCHOOL - MORNING

Students are entering the front entrance. Just up the
street. Kenny Carter stands next to ROBERT MUNSEY African
American, 18, who motions at a black male as he tries to
pass. This is STUDENT #4

                    KENNY
          Aye man, let me talk to you.

STUDENT #4 stops.

                    STUDENT #4
          What?

Kenny begins patting Student #4 pockets, he tries to resist.

                    STUDENT #4 (CONT'D)
          What are you doing man?

Robert grabs Student #4 by the lapel of his coat.

                    ROBERT MUNSEY
          What you think he's doing?

Kenny reaches into the pocket of Student #4. He pulls out a
few one-dollar bills. Robert shoves Student #4 hard, he
stumbles back.

                    ROBERT MUNSEY (CONT'D)
          Now get yo ass outta of here.

John Moon McDaniels is walking in the direction of Kenny and
Robert, he pauses and takes a good look.

Another Student is robbed as Robert aggressively takes the Student's wristwatch. John looks on as he is about to walk past, Kenny steps in front of John.

                    KENNY
          Hold it nigga.

                    JOHN
          You better get out my way nigga.

                    KENNY
          Or what.

                    JOHN
          You gon' find out fast.

The two look as though they are about to come to blows. Robert grabs Kenny.

                    ROBERT MUNSEY
          Let's deal with him later.

                    KENNY
          After school punk.

Robert and Kenny walk off. John, angry, looks on.

EXT. FREMONT HIGH SCHOOL - FOOTBALL FIELD - DAY

Dressed in school gym shorts and a gym T-shirt. Raymond is on the football field tossing the ball around with some classmates.

Raymond looks strong and fit as he runs around with the ball, throwing and catching passes. He then breaks into a routine of tumbling, displaying his gymnastic skills.

This doesn't go unnoticed by Coach VIRGIL GRANT African American male, 40.

                    VIRGIL GRANT
               (shouts)
          Raymond.

Raymond stops what he's doing. Coach Virgil Grant waves him over. Raymond breaks into a trot.

                    RAYMOND
          What's up, Coach Grant?

                    VIRGIL GRANT
          Raymond, I think you're a natural.

                    RAYMOND
          What do you mean Coach?

                    VIRGIL GRANT
          Have you thought about playing
          football?

                    RAYMOND
          Not really.

                    VIRGIL GRANT
          Why don't you try out for the team?

                    RAYMOND
          I don't think so, Coach. I just
          like foolin' around durin' gym
          class.

In the distance standing on the other side of the gate. John
Moon McDaniels waves trying to get Raymond's attention.

                    VIRGIL GRANT
          I'd hate to see all that talent go
          to waste.

Raymond notices John trying to get his attention.

                    VIRGIL GRANT (CONT'D)
          Give it some thought. You might
          change your mind.

                    RAYMOND
          I will Coach.

The bell RINGS. Raymond walks over to the gate where John is
standing.

                    RAYMOND (CONT'D)
               (teasing)
          You ditchin' sixth period.

                    JOHN
          Got problems.

                    RAYMOND
          What happened?

                    JOHN
          Kenny Carter and Robert Munsey.
          They tried to jack me up this
          morning.

                    RAYMOND
          Mutha Fucka's

                    JOHN
          Kenny said he's gon' be looking for
          me after school.

                    RAYMOND
          We run from nobody.

EXT. 78TH AND SAN PEDRO STREET - LATER

Kenny Carter, Robert Munsey, Victor Adams, Fred Stacey, Eddie
Hawthorne, and several other Avenues are loitering on the
corner. Students from the school noticeably avoid going
anywhere near the Avenues gang members.

                    KENNY
          That looks like Moon right there.

                    ROBERT MUNSEY
          He ain't alone.

                    EDDIE
          That's Raymond with him

Raymond and John are walking with purpose. They march right
up to the Avenues gang.

                    RAYMOND
          Crip here nigga.

                    KENNY
          Say what?

                    RAYMOND
          You heard me mutha fucka. What it
          be like?

                    KENNY
               (to John)
          This nigga gon' fight your battles
          for you.
               (to Raymond)
          I ain't Monson's little brother.

                    RAYMOND
          You gon' get yo ass kicked like he
          did -- Fuck him up, Moon.

Kenny sucker punches John in the face, knocking him back.

                    VICTOR
          Damn! Fired on his ass.

John quickly gathers himself. He rushes Kenny with a flurry of punches which are mostly deflected. Kenny leads with an overhand right.

John sidesteps the blow and counters with a right of his own, connecting to Kenny's jaw.

Now a large crowd of students has gathered. John exchanges blow for blow with Kenny who suddenly pulls out a PISTOL. STUDENT #5 shouts...

>   STUDENT #5
>   He's got a gun.

The students back up in a panic. TEACHER #1, out of nowhere, steps into the fray. Kenny quickly slips the pistol to Eddie who shoves it into his pocket.

>   TEACHER #1
>   Alright! Break it up! Break it
>   up!

Teacher #1 tries to restrain both Kenny and John.

>   TEACHER #1 (CONT'D)
>   Hold on you two.

Kenny snatches away from Teacher #1.

>   KENNY
>   Get yo damn hands off me.

John breaks away from the grip of Teacher #1. John and Raymond take off running.

>   KENNY (CONT'D)
>   C'mon fellas, let's get on.

Giving Teacher #1 hard looks. Kenny, Robert, Victor, Fred, Eddie, and the Avenues gang members calmly walk off. TEACHER #2 breaks through the crowd of concerned faces.

>   TEACHER #2
>   Is everything OK??

>   TEACHER #1
>   (flustered)
>   Damn gangs.

INT. HOME OF VIOLET SAMUEL - GARAGE - EVENING

A hand turns the knob on a TRANSISTOR RADIO.

MUSIC CUE: "Stand!" by Sly & The Family Stone.

Set up like a weight room. Complete with a weighted barbell,
weight plates, weight bench, dumbbells, and of course a
mirror.

Shirtless, Raymond is working out furiously, he easily bench
presses 200 pounds. Craig Craddock has two 25-pound
dumbbells in each hand.

Raymond bench presses the barbell and lays it to rest on the
bench stand. Sitting up, Raymond sits at the end of the
bench. Perspiration runs down his well define pecks and
biceps. Craig huffs and puffs, performing curls.

END MUSIC CUE:

>   CRAIG
>   Everybody's talkin' bout the fight
>   after school. How the Avenues
>   pulled a gun on you and Moon.

>   RAYMOND
>   That was a punk move.

Craig sits the dumbbells down. He walks over to his coat and
reaches into the pocket.

>   CRAIG
>   Check this out.

Raymond's eyebrows raise.

>   RAYMOND
>   Where'd you get that from?

Smiling, Craig is holding a 38 special revolver.

>   CRAIG
>   Me and some of the fellas broke
>   into a house.

>   RAYMOND
>   Breaking into houses. That's not
>   cool. That's not what a Crip is
>   about. We not like them other
>   gangs. Robbing, stealing. Niggas
>   fear us, cuz we kick ass.

>   CRAIG
>   We need a heater. Everybody don't
>   fight fair. You know that.

                    RAYMOND
          What else did you get?

                    CRAIG
          Some cash. Some jewelry.

Over the airwaves of the Transistor radio. Disc Jockey TOM
CROSS makes an announcement.

                    TOM CROSS (V.O.)
          Hey, all you KGFJ soul listeners.
          Come and have a good time at the
          Tom Cross record hop. Join me at
          Sportsman Park. I will be spinning
          all the soul sounds you love to
          groove to. That's the KGFJ Tom
          Cross record hop this Saturday at
          Sportsman Park. See you there!

INT. SPORTSMAN PARK GYMNASIUM - NIGHT

MUSIC CUE: "Mother Popcorn" by James Brown.

A huge BANNER hangs over the DJ Booth. It reads, *KGFJ Tom
Cross Record Hop*. Tom Cross, a black male in his 30s, is on
the microphone as the song "Mother Popcorn" by James Brown
plays.

                    TOM CROSS
          C'mon, get down to James Brown,
          Popcorn!

Teens and young adults are performing all the latest dances.

DJ Tom Cross looks through RECORDS, he picks one. Tom takes
the record that is spinning off the turntable.

END MUSIC CUE:

Tom puts another record on the turntable and the record
spins.

MUSIC CUE: "Baby, I'm For Real" by The Originals.

                    TOM CROSS (CONT'D)
          We gon' slow things down. So grab
          your sweetheart, hold her tight to
          The Originals, Baby, I'm For Real.

The dance floor thins out slightly as couples begin to slow
dance. As the couples grind away to the song in a passionate
embrace.

The Crip Gang members enter the scene. Led by Raymond Washington, followed by, Craig Craddock, Vertis, L.C., Elvis, Big Alden, Baby Alden, Sleepy, Ecky, and John Moon McDaniels.

Raymond checks out the scene. An attractive YOUNG LADY, African American female 17, catches his eye.

>   SLEEPY
>   (to Raymond)
>   A lot of chicks in here tonight.

>   RAYMOND
>   I got my eye on one.

The Young Lady is in a tight embrace slow dancing with another YOUNG MAN African American male, 18. With a gangsta, lean Raymond approaches the Young Lady. He completely ignores her dancing partner, the Young Man.

>   RAYMOND (CONT'D)
>   Can I have this dance?

Her dancing partner, the Young Man, is completely caught off guard. He looks at Raymond with contempt. The Young Lady is taken aback but maintains her composure and continues dancing with the Young Man.

>   YOUNG LADY
>   I'm dancing.

With a scowl on his face, Raymond addresses the Young Man.

>   RAYMOND
>   Cool if I cut in?

The Young Man steps back, he gives way. Raymond embraces the young lady closely, they begin to slow dance.

END MUSIC CUE:

EXT. SPORTSMAN PARK GYMNASIUM - NIGHT

The crowd files out of the front door. Some teens stand around smoking cigarettes. Other Young Adults linger out front talking. Raymond is with the Young Lady as they come walking out the front door entrance.

>   RAYMOND
>   I didn't mean to be so pushy.

>   YOUNG LADY
>   You're the aggressive type.

                    RAYMOND
          I can be when I need to.

                    YOUNG LADY
          What if I'd said no? I don't want
          to dance.

                    RAYMOND
          I would have just walked away.

                    YOUNG LADY
          Right, I don't believe you -- I'm
          going back inside.

                    RAYMOND
          Can I get your number before you
          go?

                    YOUNG LADY
          It was nice meeting you.

The Young Lady starts walking away.

                    RAYMOND
          It's like that?

                    YOUNG LADY
          Bye.

Several black guys in their late teens and early 20s walk up.
These are the Sportsman PARK BOYS. PARK BOYS #1 confronts
Raymond.

                    PARK BOYS #1
          You out of bounds.

                    RAYMOND
          You own this Park?

                    PARK BOYS #1
          Yeah! This is Park Boys territory.

                    RAYMOND
          That don't mean shit to me. Crip
          here nigga. I go where the fuck I
          want.

                    PARK BOYS #1
          Not tonight. You bout to get your
          ass kicked.

With a slow gangsta limp walk. Craig Craddock, Vertis, L.C.,
Elvis, Big Alden, Baby Alden, Sleepy, Ecky, and John Moon
McDaniels walk out the front entrance. They begin to chant
simultaneously...

                    CRAIG   ECKY
Crip here!   Crip Here!

                    VERTIS   ELVIS
Crip here!   Crip here!

This gets everyone's attention as the Crip gang members join
Raymond. The Crip gang, mean-mugging, is ready to face off
with the Park Boys. Park Boys #1 is not intimidated.

                    RAYMOND
          You got two choices. Join The
          Crips or get rolled over.

                    PARK BOYS #1
          You ain't gon' make it out of here
          alive.

POW! A right hand to the jaw of Park Boys #1, followed by a
left hand to the face. Park Boys #1 hits the deck. The Crip
gang mobs the Park Boys, a melee breaks out. The Crip gang
is beating down the Park Boys, mercilessly.

Several police cars roll into the park. Uniformed Officers
jump out of squad cars they race up toward the gang fight.
Pandemonium ensues, and everyone scatters including the Crip
gang members.

The police manage to wrestle several Park Boys to the ground.
Park Boys #1 takes off running. A Uniformed Officer runs him
down he's tackled, then cuffed.

EXT. FREMONT HIGH SCHOOL - GYM - DAY

INSERT CARD: SUMMER 1970

Written in black spray paint on the wall. *Chitty Chitty bang
bang, ain't nothing but a Crip thang, Crips don't die we
multiply.*

15 to 20 GANG MEMBERS wearing cuffed Levi's, khakis pants,
ducktail dress shirts, Biscuit shoes, waistline leather
coats, and Ace Duce hats file past the graffiti-laced wall.

EXT. FREMONT HIGH SCHOOL FOOTBALL FIELD - DAY

A group of 50 to 60 teenage GANG MEMBERS are seated in the bleachers. Reminiscent of a Sargent standing before his troops, Raymond Washington looks over the assembly.

> RAYMOND
> Crip here!

In unison, the response chant from the Gang Members is a resounding, CRIP HERE!

> RAYMOND (CONT'D)
> We taking over the streets of L.A.
> No other gang will stop us. I want
> the Crips to be bigger than the
> Panthers. Most of us here looked
> up to the Panthers. The pigs
> wipe'em out. The Slausons,
> Business Man, Gladiators, Outlaws,
> Rebel Rousers. Those cats are old,
> their day is over. It's a new day,
> everybody is talkin' about the new
> gang. I'm looking at the new gang -
> - Crip Here.

Again the Gang Members respond resoundingly, CRIP HERE!

> RAYMOND (CONT'D)
> We not about robbing, stealing,
> shooting people. That's not what
> we about. If somebody starts some
> shit with a Crip, we gon' finish
> it. A fink is a coward, not worthy
> to be a Crip. Remember this -- a
> Crip, is a Crip for life.

EXT. CAMP ROCKEY SAN DIMAS CALIFORNIA - EXERCISE AREA - DAY

MUSIC CUE: "Get Down" by Curtis Mayfield.

A group of African American male youths is congregated together. Among them is STANLEY TOOKIE WILLIAMS 17, a male African American. He is lifting weights with several other well-built African American male youths.

White and Mexican youths are segregated. The grumbling of racial descent spews from the mouths of various ethnic groups.

A BLACK GUY, 17, stands with his peers as he trades insults with white and Mexican inmates.

END MUSIC CUE:

> BLACK GUY
> You white devils, fuckin' wetbacks.

Within earshot, a WHITE GUY, 17, is huddled with his kind.

> WHITE GUY
> You nigger!

Likewise, a MEXICAN GUY, 17, stands strong with his homeboys.

> MEXICAN GUY
> Fuck you mayate!

With a scowl on his face, buffed up Tookie sporting 17-inch biceps, walks around with his chest raised up, arms out to the side.

INT. CAMP ROCKEY SAN DIMAS CALIFORNIA - DORM ROOM - NIGHT

Steel bunks line both sides of a slightly elevated control center where a male COUNSELLOR stands vigil. The Counsellor steps away from his post.

Four WHITE MALE youths and a MALE MEXICAN youth ambush an unsuspecting MALE BLACK youth that lies in his bunk. Blankets are thrown over his head, the Black Youth is beaten senseless.

Far in the back lying in a bunk next to the wall, Tookie listens, as he hears the moans and thuds that come from the beaten Black Youth.

INT. CAMP ROCKEY SAN DIMAS CALIFORNIA - KITCHEN - DAY

Hairnet on his head, Tookie is preparing meals. He pushes a cart filled with food trays to the cafeteria when he is stopped by COUNSELLOR #1.

> COUNSELLOR #1
> Stanley, head over to the gym. The
> staff wants to talk with you.

> TOOKIE
> Alright.

INT. CAMP ROCKEY SAN DIMAS CALIFORNIA - GYM - CONTINUOUS

Tookie walks in, he takes a seat before a staff tribunal.
Seated opposite Tookie are STAFF MEMBER #1, STAFF MEMBER #2,
and STAFF MEMBER #3.

> STAFF MEMBER #1
> Stanley, you have been summoned
> here for a customary re-evaluation.

Tookie is stoned-faced no smiles. Staff Member #1 opens up a
FOLDER, looks over several DOCUMENTS.

> STAFF MEMBER #1 (CONT'D)
> We want each youth that enters this
> camp to leave a better person.

> STAFF MEMBER #2
> For the most part, you've managed
> to stay out of trouble. A couple
> of skirmishes, but nothing serious.

> STAFF MEMBER #3
> How do you like working in the
> kitchen? You're the head cook.

Tookie shrugs his shoulders.

> TOOKIE
> It's alright.

> STAFF MEMBER #1
> Stanley, what are your plans once
> you're released?

Tookie ponders for a moment.

> TOOKIE
> I'm gon' hook up with a gang.
> (emphasize)
> I wanna be a gang leader.

The Staff Members look puzzled. Tookie gets out of the
chair, he swaggers off leaving the Staff Members looking
baffled.

EXT. CAMP ROCKEY SAN DIMAS CALIFORNIA - GATE - DAY

INSERT CARD: TWO DAYS LATER

Tookie is standing out front, with a duffle bag at his side.
A car pulls up, and Tookie grabs his duffle bag and gets in.

INT. CAR - CONTINUOUS

An African American man in his late 30s sits behind the
wheel, this is FRED HOLIWELL. He stares at Tookie through
the rearview mirror.

                    FRED
          How you doin' Stanley? It's good
          to see you.

Tookie with a serious look...

                    TOOKIE
          I'm OK.

An African American woman, 34, is sitting in the front
passenger seat. This is Tookie's mother LOUISIANA WILLIAMS,
she turns to face him.

                    LOUISIANA WILLIAMS
          Hey baby, I've missed you. I know
          you happy to get out of that place.

                    TOOKIE
          Yeah, Mama. Let's get out of here.

Tookie is sitting in the back seat when the car pulls off,
and he doesn't look back. Camp Rockey in the background,
grows small in the distance.

EXT. APARTMENT BUILDING SOUTH LOS ANGELES - DAY

Tookie is standing with RICARDO BUB SIMS African American
male 17, and TERRY African American male 17. They
enthusiastically give Tookie the black handshake.

                    BUB
          You didn't snitch man.

                    TERRY
          Yeah, you stayed down homeboy.

                    TOOKIE
          I wasn't gon' give you guys up.

Terry notices Tookie's bulging arms.

                    TERRY
          You got buffed up in camp.

                    BUB
          You all yoked up.

                         TOOKIE
         Eight months, eating and driving
         iron.

                         BUB
         Aye man, thanks again for not
         snitching.

                         TOOKIE
         Forget it, man. I don't wanna talk
         about that shit.

                         TERRY
         Streets ain't changed much. A few
         older gangs still trying to hang
         on. Some new gangs popped up.
         Sportsman Park Boys, Denker Boys,
         Manchester Park Boys, Hustler Mob,
         New House Boys.

                         TOOKIE
         Being kicked out of different
         schools. In and outta juvenile
         hall, different camps. Moms moving
         all over L.A. I got cool with
         niggas from different gangs. A lot
         of cats respect me. It's time to
         band together. We need to be
         prepared to deal with any gang that
         comes at us.

MONTAGE.

EXT. RESIDENTIAL STREET - NIGHT

Tookie is with Terry and Bub, using a SLIM JIM they break
into a car.

INT. CAR - CONTINUOUS

A SNATCH BAR rips out the ignition.

EXT. RIVAL GANG TERRITORY - NIGHT

Cruising in the car, it comes to a sudden stop. Tookie,
Terry, and Bub bail out of the car. They beat down an
unsuspecting GANG MEMBER.

EXT. LOCAL HIGH SCHOOL - DAY

Tookie is furiously beating up a GANG MEMBER as students look
on.

EXT. LIQUOR STORE - SOUTH LOS ANGELES - DAY

Tookie, Terry, and Bub attack two GANG MEMBERS coming out.

EXT. ALLEY - NIGHT

A GANG MEMBER is scrawling graffiti on a garage wall. Tookie
snatches the spray paint can from the Gang Member. Terry and
Bub beat the Gang Member mercilessly.

END OF MONTAGE.

I/E. APARTMENT BUILDING SOUTH LOS ANGELES - NIGHT

A CAR slowly pulls up with four BLACK YOUTHS in it. In the
back seat, BLACK YOUTH #1 is pointing.

                    BLACK YOUTH #1
              That's it right there.

Black Youth #1 gets out, he cautiously looks around. Holding
a spray paint can, he then scrawls on the wall. *We gonna
kill you Tookie.*

EXT. WASHINGTON HIGH SCHOOL - EVENING

Establishing shot of the MARQUEE. The echo of concerned
VOICES can be heard.

INT. WASHINGTON HIGH SCHOOL AUDITORIUM - CONTINUOUS

Parents are animated. A meeting is underway, the POLICE and
school ADMINISTRATORS are in attendance. Frustrated, PARENT
#1 lodges a complaint.

                    PARENT #1
              He's causing trouble on and off
              campus!

PARENT #2 erupts.

                    PARENT #2
          Who is this Kid? Do you know
          anything about him?

ADMINISTRATOR #1 holding his hands up attempts to quell
fears.

                    ADMINISTRATOR #1
          Look, we have a handle on the
          situation.

                    PARENT #1
          Handle my ass. You're clueless
          about what's happening in this
          school.

A Police Officer, SARGENT MORRIS male white 45, intervenes.

                    SARGENT MORRIS
          My name is Sargent Morris. I'm
          with LAPD 77th Division. The
          description we have is that this
          kid is dark-skinned, with a scar on
          his face, and very muscular.

PARENT #3 rises out of the seat.

                    PARENT #3
          This boy is recruiting kids to join
          his gang. He's using fear to do
          it. Now he's after my son. The
          kids that attend this school know
          who he is -- They call him Tookie.

EXT. TERRY'S HOUSE - DAY

Sitting around the porch are Terry, ERSKINE JONES African
American male, 17, and Tookie. They're in the midst of a
jovial conversation.

                    TERRY
          So what do you think about that
          name?

                    TOOKIE
          I don't know man. That takes some
          getting used to.

                    TERRY
          "Bimbo," that's my nickname. Yeah,
          I like it, Bimbo.

Tookie looks at Terry oddly, he begins to chuckle.

                    TOOKIE
          Erskine, what you think?

Terry looks somewhat annoyed.

                    TERRY
          I insist on being called Bimbo.

                    ERSKINE
          I like it. I think it sounds cool.

A big smile appears on Terry's face.

                    TERRY
          See, that's what I'm saying.

                    ERSKINE
          I should have a nickname.

                    TOOKIE
          Aw shit.

Tookie looks at Terry.

                    TOOKIE (CONT'D)
               (jokingly)
          Terry, see what you done started.

                    TERRY
          What should we call you? Does it
          have to do with crazy? Cuz, you
          crazy nigga. You'll fly off the
          handle at any time.

                    TOOKIE
          I know -- Mad Dog! A Mad Dog is
          crazy. That's what we gon' call
          you.

                    ERSKINE
          I love it.

Erskine proudly struts around.

                    ERSKINE (CONT'D)
          Yeah, I'm Mad Dog, I'll knock a
          mutha fucka out. I'll kill a mutha
          fucka.

Erskine then notices that Tookie and Terry's left ears are
pierced. A small piece of STRAW sticks out of both their
ears which have been swabbed with Vaseline.

                         ERSKINE (CONT'D)
          What's that in y'all ear?

Erskine examines both Tookie's and Terry's ears.

                         TOOKIE
          It's our new style.

                         ERSKINE
          Ah, straw in your ear?

                         TOOKIE
          The straw is temporary fool. I'll
          replace it with an earring. It's
          about image. I want to set myself
          apart from other gangs. African
          warriors pierce their ears and
          noses.

                         ERSKINE
          I'm a warrior, but I'm not from
          Africa. I don't need an earring.

                         TOOKIE
          Whatever man.

                         TERRY
          Other gangs don't give a damn about
          image. Some of the gangs want
          peace, other gangs want war.

                         TOOKIE
          I'm hooking up with cats that I'm
          cool with. Squabblin' with every
          gang we run into won't work.
          That's a mistake other gangs make --
          not us.

EXT. WASHINGTON HIGH SCHOOL - QUAD AREA - DAY

INSERT CARD: SPRING 1971

MUSIC CUE: "Smiling Faces Sometimes" by The Undisputed Truth.

It's lunchtime, students are all about. Some are sitting on
the grass. Others just kick back hanging out.

Tookie is strolling down the concrete walkway when he notices
two strangers headed his way. They are clearly looking for
Tookie as he braces himself for trouble.

Both strangers are extremely muscular, it's Raymond
Washington and BENNIE RAY BULLDOG SIMPSON, African American
male 18.

END MUSIC CUE:

                    RAYMOND
          Hey Tookie!

Raymond and Bulldog approach Tookie. Raymond stands within
arm's length of Tookie. Bulldog stands beside Raymond.

                    RAYMOND (CONT'D)
          Are you Tookie?

                    TOOKIE
          Yeah, I'm Tookie, why?

Tookie notices a scar running upward from the corner of
Raymond's mouth.

FLASHBACK:

EXT. EAST SIDE SOUTH LOS ANGELES - STREET - DAY

Raymond Washington is fighting furiously with Craig Monson.
Raymond is punched in the face by Craig. He falls on his
back, and BLOOD seeps from Raymond's cheek.

END FLASHBACK:

EXT. WASHINGTON HIGH SCHOOL - QUAD AREA - DAY

Bulldog, looking stern stands next to Raymond as he extends
his right hand. Tookie cautiously looks at Raymond.

                    RAYMOND
          I'm Raymond Washington, that's
          Bulldog.

Tookie nods, acknowledging both of them.

                    RAYMOND (CONT'D)
          You know Clint?

                    TOOKIE
          Yeah, I know Clint.

                    RAYMOND
          Cuz told me how you stand up to
          other gangs. Even when you
          outnumber. I have to deal with the
          same shit on the east side.

Tookie with an indifferent look on his face just stands
there.

                    RAYMOND (CONT'D)
          I need cats like you in my gang.

Tookie notices the way Raymond and Bulldog are dressed. They
are all dressed similarly. Heavily starched cuffed Levi's,
black biscuit shoes, black waistline leather coats. With the
exception of Tookie's wide-brim hat.

                    TOOKIE
          I hate gangs. I want to crush
          them. But -- I'll give it some
          thought. Meet me at the Rio
          Theater Sunday.

I/E. RIO THEATER - DAY

INSERT CARD: SUNDAY

As they recline in their seats. The reflection of light from
the movie screen dimly illuminates the faces of several black
teens --

Tookie, Mad Dog Erskine, Ricardo Bub Sims, DONALD SWEETBACK
ARCHIE African American male 17, JAMES CUZZ CUNNINGHAM
African American male 17, LURCH African American male 18,
Terry Bimbo, and BOB BIG HAWK CREAR African American male 19.

The THEATER MANAGER taps Tookie on his shoulder.

                    THEATER MANAGER
          Aye, man. There's a bunch of ruff-
          looking dudes standing out front.
          One of'em asked for you.

Tookie gets out of his seat. He walks up the dark aisle with
the Theater Manager.

Raymond is standing outside with some of his homeboys. He
sees Tookie enter the lobby as he walks up to the glass door
opening it. Peering out...

                    TOOKIE
          What's up cuz? C'mon in.

Raymond looks slightly puzzled.

                    RAYMOND
          Cuz, we ain't got enough money to
          get everybody in.

                    TOOKIE
          Don't worry bout it.

Raymond files in with FERNANDO PA PA SIMS African American
male 18, ROBERT DUHON African American male 16, Ecky, LITTLE
SAM African American male 17, RAYMOND CHILI LEWIS African
American male 17, and DEADEYE CLINT WILLIS African American
male 18.

                    RAYMOND
          These mah homeboys.

Standing in the LOBBY they acknowledge Tookie with head nods.

                    RAYMOND (CONT'D)
          Fernando, Duhon, Ecky, Little Sam.
          That's Chili, you know Clint.

                    CLINT
          What up Tookie.

                    TOOKIE
          What's up cuz? Let's go inside.

The reflection of light from the movie screen shines dimly.
Raymond's homeboys sit down in front. Tookie and Raymond sit
next to each other.

                    TOOKIE (CONT'D)
          I'm gon' hook up with you. Yo,
          homeboys and mines. No gang will
          be able to stop us.

Nodding his head, Raymond listens intently.

                    TOOKIE (CONT'D)
          Meet me at Washington High Friday.
          Bring as many dudes as you can.
          I'll have all my homeboys there.
          We'll seal the deal then.

EXT. WASHINGTON HIGH SCHOOL - DAY

INSERT CARD: FRIDAY

The school BELL RINGS. Standing around the football
bleachers, Raymond Washington is with 30 of his HOMEBOYS.
Bub stands next to a perplexed-looking Tookie.

                    RAYMOND
          What's happenin'? Where yo
          homeboys?

                    TOOKIE
          They'll be here.

Craig Craddock steps out from amongst the crowd.

                    CRAIG
          Tookie, is that them?

Tookie turns around to see the grand entrance.

MUSIC CUE: "Get Up And Get Down" by The Dramatics.

A smiling Terry "Bimbo" is strolling across the football
field with of throng of his homeboys.

                    TOOKIE
                 (radiant)
          That's some of'em.

Then, strolling in from the northeast side of the bleachers,
Lurch is leading a horde of his homeboys. Tookie's face is
filled with pride.

They are dressed in a wide variety of styles. Beige khaki
suits, starched Levi's, black leather coats, silk suits, army
boots, black biscuits, suit coat vests, and wooden canes.

Gathered around the bleachers is a large group of young black
gang members. They represent a small division of reckless,
energetic, and fearless young warriors.

Raymond and Tookie shake hands and embrace. A deafening and
primal roar can be heard from their homeboys signifying their
approval.

END MUSIC CUE:

INT. APARTMENT BUILDING - TOOKIE'S ROOM - MORNING

Tookie is lying in his bed asleep. His mother Louisiana
Williams walks in.

                    LOUISIANA WILLIAMS
          Stanley get up, it's two o'clock.
          You gon' sleep in all day?

Tookie is slow to wake, his mother shakes him. She is
shocked to discover the pillow under his head is soaked with
blood. Tookie's mother shakes him vigorously.

                    LOUISIANA WILLIAMS (CONT'D)
          Stanley, Stanley. Wake-up boy.

Tookie begins to rouse from his slumber.

                    TOOKIE
          What?

                    LOUISIANA WILLIAMS
          There's blood all over your pillow.

Tookie's mother Louisiana Williams examines his head. There
is a laceration on Tookie's right ear.

                    LOUISIANA WILLIAMS (CONT'D)
          This looks bad. I'm gon' have to
          take you to the hospital.

INT. HOSPITAL - EMERGENCY ROOM - DAY

Tookie is sitting upright on the bed while being stitched up
by the DOCTOR. Louisiana Williams is clearly angry.

                    LOUISIANA WILLIAMS
          You just got out of camp, and you
          get right back into trouble.

Tookie has a look of dread as his mother's voice fades...

                    LOUISIANA WILLIAMS (CONT'D)
          I can't keep doing this, you hear
          me...

FLASHBACK:

EXT. GYMNASIUM - NIGHT

A dance is underway it's packed with people. Raymond and
Tookie are engaged in conversation with two YOUNG WOMEN. A
huge GANG MEMBER standing six foot eight inches tall enters
the scene.

The Gang Member is with some of his homeboys they approach
Raymond and Tookie. Words are exchanged, and everyone's body
language displays a demeanor of hostility.

Without warning Raymond and Tookie hit the Gang Member at the
same time, and he stumbles back. Tookie in a rage punches
the Gang Member several more times, and he staggers. Raymond
runs up to the Gang Member unleashing body shots.

Tookie is just about to punch the Gang Member again when he
is blind-sided. He's hit with a metal folding chair that
knocks him backward.

Tookie dazed, is laid out on the floor. Raymond helps Tookie
to his feet, and blood seeps from his ear. A troop of Crip
gang members comes to their aid, beating up the Gang Member
and his homeboys.

END FLASHBACK:

INT. HOSPITAL - EMERGENCY ROOM - DAY

Thread looping through Tookie's ear. The Doctor is still
applying sutures as Tookie's mother paces the floor.

                    TOOKIE
          That's what happened.

                    LOUISIANA WILLIAMS
          Are you the same child I gave birth
          to? Or were you switched at birth?

                    DOCTOR
          Whelp, that's it. Ten sutures.

The Doctor applies a medical dressing to Tookie's ear.

                    DOCTOR (CONT'D)
          He'll be fine.

EXT. WASHINGTON HIGH SCHOOL - LUNCH AREA - DAY

Sitting around tables. Mad Dog Erskine, Terry Bimbo, and
Lurch are in the midst of a lively debate. Tookie,
indifferent, kicks back. Raymond Washington, a dismissive
look, just listens.

                    TERRY
          Black Crusaders.

                    ERSKINE
Mau-Maus.

                    BIMBO
I got one -- The Eliminators.

                    LURCH
Nah man, what about this? The
Terminators. What do you think
Tookie?

                    TOOKIE
        (nonchalant)
The name Tookie is gon' overshadow
any gang name we pick.

                    ERSKINE
        (sarcastic)
So what? We should call ourselves
the Tookies?

Raymond interjects.

                    RAYMOND
Crip!

                    BIMBO
Say what?

                    LURCH
Crip, what the hell is that?

                    RAYMOND
The name of the gang. I came up
with the name two years ago.

                    ERSKINE
        (ponder)
Crip, huh.

                    TOOKIE
It don't matter to me, man. My
name speaks for itself.

EXT. BONNIE QUARLES HOUSE - GARAGE - BACKYARD - NIGHT

MUSIC CUE: "Somebody's Watching You" by Little Sister.

A party is going on. BONNIE QUARLES female, African American
17, is visibly upset. She weaves through the crowd of
TEENAGERS. Bonnie rushes up to Tookie as he walks in.

END MUSIC CUE:

                 BONNIE
Tookie, some niggas came up in the
party tryin' to start some shit.

                 TOOKIE
Oh yeah, where they at?

                 BONNIE
I don't know. They left a little
while ago.

Looking tuff, grouped around Tookie is Terry Bimbo, Lurch,
and Mad Dog Erskine. Just then, the troublemakers are back.

MUSIC CUE: "The Underground" by Curtis Mayfield.

With a scowl on his face is CURTIS BUDDHA MORROW, male
African American, 16. Standing next to him is MONKEY MAN,
16, a lanky-looking African American male.

Both teens are clearly inebriated, Bonnie exclaims...

                 BONNIE (CONT'D)
That's them right there.

Tookie, Terry Bimbo, Lurch, Mad Dog Erskine quickly confront
the two.

                 TOOKIE
Tonight's not yo night.

                 BUDDHA
We gon' turn this mutha fucka out.

                 TOOKIE
You bout to get fucked up.

                 MONKEY MAN
Fuck you and this party.

END MUSIC CUE:

Buddha throws the first punch at Tookie. His mistake, Tookie
works him over. Monkey Man jumps in, his mistake. Terry
Bimbo, Lurch, and Mad Dog Erskine have their way with him.

The party is now a spectator sport, Bonnie and her guest can
only watch the brawl. Both Buddha and Monkey Man are beaten
up, then tossed out onto the street.

EXT. WASHINGTON HIGH SCHOOL - CAFETERIA - MORNING

Tookie is in the breakfast line when he is approached by
Buddha and Monkey Man. Tookie is hardly phased.

                    TOOKIE
          Y'all back for more?

Buddha and Monkey Man are quickly surrounded by Terry Bimbo,
Bub, Mad Dog Erskine, James Cuzz Cunningham, and Lurch.
Buddha and Monkey Man recognize that they are outnumbered.

                    BUDDHA
          We not here for a fight.

                    TOOKIE
          Then what the fuck you want?

                    MONKEY MAN
          It's cool man. We want to join up
          with you.

                    TOOKIE
          This ain't the army nigga.

                    MONKEY MAN
          You looking for soldiers, right?

                    TOOKIE
          Maybe.

                    BUDDHA
          Then we want to be down.

                    TOOKIE
          I guess if y'all crazy enough to
          crash ma girl's party. You crazy
          enough to join my gang -- I'm
          Tookie.

                    BUDDHA
          We know who you are. They call me
          Buddha. This is my homeboy, Monkey
          Man.

                    TOOKIE
          Alright -- Buddha, Monkey Man.
          Y'all can be down with us.

They all give each other the black handshake.

EXT. INGLEWOOD FORUM - NIGHT

The MARQUEE says *JACKSON 5* in concert tonight. The parking
lot is full of cars.

EXT. RESIDENTIAL NEIGHBORHOOD - STREET - NIGHT

A CAR is parked. Four young people get out: BLACK MALE #1,
BLACK WOMAN #1, BLACK MALE #2, and BLACK WOMAN #2. They're
all dressed up, BLACK MALE #1 looking like Superfly, is
wearing a leather MAXI COAT.

BLACK MALE #2, perfectly shaped afro, polyester print shirt,
knit slacks, waistline leather coat. BLACK WOMAN #1 is
putting on LIPSTICK. She turns to BLACK WOMAN #2.

                    BLACK WOMAN #1
          How's my lipstick look, girl?

                    BLACK WOMAN #2
          You look fine.

Looking at the girls, Black Male #2 pats his afro.

                    BLACK MALE #2
          How mah afro look?

Black Male #1 is anxious.

                    BLACK MALE #1
          Man, not you too. C'mon let's go,
          we gon' be late for the concert.

As they begin to walk. Tookie and Buddha come out of
nowhere.

                    TOOKIE
          Give up the coats.

                    BLACK MALE #2
          What? You got to be jivin'.

                    TOOKIE
          You think so.

                    BLACK MALE #2
          You better be.

Tookie suddenly levels Black Male #2 with a thunderous blow.
He's on his back out cold. Black Male #1, completely
intimidated, takes off his coat. Tookie gestures to Buddha.

                    TOOKIE
          Get that dude's coat. Take the
          broad's purses.

                    BLACK WOMAN #1
          Aye man, this shit ain't cool.

                    TOOKIE
          Shut the fuck up.

Putting up no resistance. Buddha takes the purses from Black
Woman #1 and Black Woman #2, and the coat from Black Male #1.
Tookie takes the coat off an unconscious Black Male #2.

Tookie then runs through his pockets taking whatever money he
finds. Tookie looks up at Buddha, and with a nod, they trot
off into the dark.

                    BLACK WOMAN #2
          I told y'all we should have parked
          in the parking lot.

MONTAGE:

EXT. INGLEWOOD FORUM - PARKING LOT - NIGHT

Mad Dog Erskine and Monkey Man strong-arm a MAN of his
leather coat. Terrified, a LADY can only watch as Donald
Sweetback Archie and Lurch beat and rob two male teens.

TEENAGER #1 is excited, he shows TEENAGER #2 his TICKETS.
Suddenly Cuzz Cunningham snatches the tickets from the hand
of TEENAGER #1, then BIG BUNCHIE male African American, 17,
fiercely slaps him.

We see several PEOPLE running as CRIPS gang members are in
pursuit.

END OF MONTAGE:

EXT. SOUTH LOS ANGELES - MANCHESTER BLVD - NIGHT

As if in a parade, a celebratory march is underway. 100 Crip
Gang Members, led by Tookie, are very animated.

Cruising slowly, five cars loaded with BLACK MEN are trailing
the Crip gang members. This is the CHAIN GANG, they pull
alongside the Crip Gang members. From one of the cars, CHAIN
GANG MEMBER #1 hangs out the front side passenger window.

                    CHAIN GANG MEMBER #1
                Fuck the Crips! This is Chain Gang
                mutha fucka!

The Crip gang members come to an abrupt stop. They all begin
to yell CRIP HERE, simultaneously throwing up their gang
sign, forming the letter "C", with the index finger and
thumb.

GUNSHOTS RING OUT. The Crip gang members scramble for cover.
Running frantically, they make their way into a nearby park.

EXT. ST. ANDREWS PARK - NIGHT

Some with frayed nerves, others undaunted. Crip gang members
are hiding amongst the dimly lit trees, tabletops, benches,
swings, and playground area. Tookie surveys the situation.

                        TOOKIE
                    (pronounced)
                Everybody be cool.

About 20 Chain Gang members lurk in the dark ready for
action. Chain Gang Member #1 cuffs both hands around his
mouth, resembling a megaphone.

                    CHAIN GANG MEMBER #1
                    (loudly)
                Tookie. Let's get down right now.
                A fight, the Chain Gang against the
                Crips.

                        TOOKIE
                You niggas are cowards. Bunch ah
                grown men using guns against
                teenagers.

                    CHAIN GANG MEMBER #1
                No Guns. We ready to fight. The
                Crips can't come to Inglewood
                robbing and beating people up.

Buddha and Mad Dog Erskine step out of the shadows.

                        BUDDHA
                    (shouts)
                Chain Gang. Bring yo ass out here.
                We ready mutha fucka.

                        ERSKINE
                Crip here!

                    CHAIN GANG MEMBER #1
          (shouts)
     Bring it on then.

The Crip gang members led by Buddha and Mad Dog Erskine,
mobilize. Tookie comes out of the shadows, with him are
Monkey Man, Lurch, Terry Bimbo, Big Bunchie and Cuzz
Cunningham, and Donald Sweetback Archie.

GUNSHOTS RING OUT. The Crip gang members sprint off into the
dark. Running in different directions, some dart across
Manchester Blvd and into a car dealership.

EXT. CAR DEALERSHIP - CONTINUOUS

Bullets ricochet, ducking behind brand new CARS, using them
as cover. Tookie, Buddha, Mad Dog Erskine, Donald Sweetback
Archie, Monkey Man, Big Bunchie, and Lurch collect
themselves.

                    TOOKIE
     Man, we trapped.

                    BUDDHA
     We gotta get outta here.

A carload of black guys pull up, it's the Chain Gang. Chain
Gang Member #1 looks out of the back passenger window.

                    CHAIN GANG MEMBER #1
     We got yo ass now Tookie.

Brandishing a REVOLVER, Chain Gang Member #1 is ready to take
aim. Just then Buddha comes from behind a car firing shots
from a 38 PISTOL.

Chain Gang Member #1 ducks down. The car is pelted with
projectiles as the tires screech. Mad Dog Erskine, arm
raised, PISTOL in hand, pops out from behind a car.

He starts busting off rounds as he joins Buddha. The Chain
Gang speeds off the back window of their car shatter.

                    TOOKIE
     Let's bail before they come back.

Tookie, Lurch, and, Donald Sweetback Archie are trapped
between a wall and several cars. Bunchie is cowering, and
crying, and has blocked their path.

                    TOOKIE (CONT'D)
     Bunchie, move man!

                    BIG BUNCHIE
I can't.

                    TOOKIE
You gon' get us killed, <u>move</u>.

Big Bunchie, terrified, will not budge. With one mighty kick
from Lurch, Big Bunchie rolls over. Lurch leaps over Big
Bunchie, he breaks out running. Right behind him are Tookie
and Donald Sweetback Archie.

INSERT CARD: RETRIBUTION

INT. HOUSE - CHAIN GANG HANG OUT - DAY

MUSIC CUE: "Family Affair" by Sly & The Family Stone.

Chain Gang members dance and smoke weed with their HOMEGIRLS.
Chain Gang Member #1, smiling, takes a long drag from a
marijuana cigarette.

Sitting in a corner. CHAIN GANG MEMBER #2, holding a
marijuana cigarette, takes a sip from a can of beer. High,
he slightly bobs his head to the music.

                  CHAIN GANG MEMBER #2
      Check this out. We need to come up
      with a new name. The Chain Gang is
      played out, you old cats came up
      with that name.

                  CHAIN GANG MEMBER #1
      Say what?

                  CHAIN GANG MEMBER #2
      We one big Family.

Chain Gang Member #1 takes another drag from the marijuana
cigarette. He inhales, and his chest expands.

                  CHAIN GANG MEMBER #1
        (holding breath)
      Family, I like that.
        (blows smoke out his
         mouth)
      Inglewood Family -- From now on we
      are called, Inglewood Family.

END MUSIC CUE:

EXT. HOUSE - CHAIN GANG HANG OUT - DAY

Crip gang members are encamped around the premises. BIG
CURTIS African American male, 17, FAT RILEY African American
male, 17, and Raymond Washington are crouched at the front
door. Raymond looks at Big Curtis and Fat Riley.

                    RAYMOND
          On three. One, two, three.

BAM! They kick in the front door, and rush in, followed by a
host of Crip gang members. VOICES are raised, SHOUTING,
CURSING, the music comes to an abrupt halt, and the SOUND of
a needle stretching a record is heard.

FURNITURE CRACKING, GLASS BREAKING, two CHAIN GANG MEMBERS
fly out of the front WINDOW. Chain Gang members rush out the
back door.

Waiting on them are a slew of Crip gang members. They
commence to beat down the Chain Gang members, fist-slamming
into jaws, and CANES upside the head. Vastly outnumbered,
the Chain Gang is completely overrun by Crip gang members.

EXT. WILL ROGERS PARK - DAY

INSERT CARD: WATTS FESTIVAL SUMMER 1971

The atmosphere is full of Black Pride. Throngs of BLACK
PEOPLE sporting DASHIKI'S, AFRO'S, and African style
CORNROWS, watch the PARADE proceed down CENTRAL AVENUE.

Raymond has shown up with over 100 Crip gang members
accompanying him. Like two army platoons meeting up.
Tookie, too, with an equal number of Crip gang members,
greets Raymond.

                    TOOKIE
          What's happenin' cuz.

                    RAYMOND
          From the Watts riot to the Watts
          festival. Eastside to the
          Westside.

Standing around Raymond is MAC THOMAS, a muscular light-
complexion African American male, 18, and BLACK JOHNNY
African American male, 18.

                    RAYMOND (CONT'D)
          This is Mac Thomas. He runs the
          Compton Crips.
                    (MORE)

                    RAYMOND (CONT'D)
This mah homeboy Black Johnny. He
started the 43rd Street Crips.

Tookie shakes their hands.

                    MAC THOMAS
          Sup.

                    BLACK JOHNNY
          Sup.

                    TOOKIE
We getting bigger and bigger cuz.

                    RAYMOND
Everybody knows about the Crips.
Cats from all over the city wanna
join the Crips.

                    TOOKIE
Look at all the Crips out here at
the festival. This is some major
shit cuz.

                    RAYMOND
          (proud)
Yeah, it is.

Like a feeling-out party, the mass of Crip gang members
interact amongst each other.

EXT. CENTENNIAL HIGH - EVENING

INSERT CARD: OCTOBER 1971

Establishing shot of the MARQUEE. A YELLOW SCHOOL BUS pulls
up. The football team still in uniform steps off the bus.
ZANE SMITH African American male, 17, is approached by the
COACH.

                    COACH
Zane, you played a good game.
Theirs some things we need to work
on.

                    ZANE
Sure, coach.

INT. CENTENNIAL HIGH - BOYS LOCKER ROOM - EVENING

Creeping around is a group of teens. A.C. Moses, LORENZO
BENTON African American male 17, LARRY TAM WATTS African
American male 17, LIL VINCE OWENS African American male 17,
and SYLVESTER PUDDIN' SCOTT African American male 17.

They break into several lockers taking personal items, coats,
watches, and money.

A.C. pries open a locker with a SCREWDRIVER. He pulls out a
nice LEATHER COAT, eyes it, then continues to ramble through
the locker.

A DOOR opens, and the football team is entering. VOICES can
be heard, this alerts A.C.

                    A.C.
          Aye, let's get out of here.

EXT. CENTENNIAL HIGH - BOYS LOCKER ROOM - CONTINUOUS

The exit DOOR flies open. A.C., Lorenzo, Tam, Vince, and
Puddin' come racing out with stolen leather coats.

EXT. PIRU STREET - RESIDENTIAL NEIGHBORHOOD - NIGHT

INSERT CARD: COMPTON, CALIFORNIA

The road sign PIRU STREET stand out prominently.

MUSIC CUE: "Inner City Blues" by Marvin Gaye.

We follow the music as it leads us to a house. Teenagers are
mingling out front, and through the window, a silhouette of
people is seen dancing inside.

END MUSIC CUE:

INT. HOUSE - CONTINUOUS

A HAND drops the NEEDLE on a 45 RECORD.

MUSIC CUE: "Rock Steady" by Aretha Franklin.

TEENS and YOUNG ADULTS are dancing. A.C., Lorenzo, Tam, Lil
Vince, and Puddin' stroll in the door. With them is CRAZY
JAMES EDDIE, African American male 17. He is wearing the
LEATHER COAT that A.C. had stolen.

Two observant teens notice the leather coat that Crazy James Eddie has on. This is CRIP GANG MEMBER #1 and CRIP GANG MEMBER #2.

END MUSIC CUE:

> CRIP GANG MEMBER #1
> Check out that jacket cuz got on.

> CRIP GANG MEMBER #2
> I see.

> CRIP GANG MEMBER #1
> Look familiar to you?

> CRIP GANG MEMBER #2
> Yeah, it does.

> CRIP GANG MEMBER #1
> C'mon.

Crazy James Eddie, enjoying the lively atmosphere when he is confronted by the two Crip Gang Members. Their demeanor isn't in the least bit friendly.

> CRIP GANG MEMBER #1 (CONT'D)
> What's up cuz?

Crazy James Eddie is taken aback, he looks at the two Crip Gang Members suspiciously.

> CRAZY JAMES EDDIE
> What's up?

> CRIP GANG MEMBER #1
> Where you get that jacket from?

> CRAZY JAMES EDDIE
> Why?

A.C., ear hustling is standing a few feet away.

> CRIP GANG MEMBER #2
> You know Zane Smith? He plays
> football for Centennial.

> CRAZY JAMES EDDIE
> So.

> CRIP GANG MEMBER #1
> That's his jacket you're wearing.

                    CRAZY JAMES EDDIE
          This my mutha fucken' jacket.
          Ain't nothing gon' change that.

                    CRIP GANG MEMBER #1
          Come off the jacket cuz.

                    CRAZY JAMES EDDIE
          Fuck you.

A.C. interjects.

                    A.C.
          What's happenin'?

                    CRAZY JAMES EDDIE
          This mutha fucka saying mah jacket,
          ain't mah jacket.

Lorenzo, Tam, Lil Vince, and Puddin' walk in on the
situation. They sense things are tense.

                    TAM
          Everything cool.

                    CRAZY JAMES EDDIE
          These cats think my jacket belongs
          to their homeboy.

Tam, straight-faced, turns to the two Crip Gang Members.

                    TAM
          Mah homeboy says it's his jacket.
          It's his jacket.

                    CRIP GANG MEMBER #2
          Bullshit! That's Zane Smith's
          jacket.

Some people in the party recognize that there is friction
between both gang factions.

                    CRAZY JAMES EDDIE
          We can take this shit outside.

                    CRIP GANG MEMBER #1
          Ain't no thang cuz.

Crazy James Eddie angrily storms out the front door. On his
heels is Crip Gang Member #1, followed by Crip Gang Member
#2. Right behind them, A.C., Lorenzo, Tam, Lil Vince, and
Puddin' rush out ready for battle.

EXT. HOUSE PARTY - CONTINUOUS

Crazy James Eddie runs over to a CAR. He opens the trunk and
pulls out a BUMPER JACK. Crazy James Eddie turns toward Crip
Gang Member #1, and Crip Gang Member #2.

> CRIP GANG MEMBER #1
> What the fuck you gon' do with
> that?

Crazy James Eddie rears back with the bumper jack. He runs
up on Crip Gang Member #1 swinging recklessly, who dodges the
attempted blows.

Crip Gang Member #2 takes a swing at Crazy James Eddie who
turns the bumper jack loose on him. Like a matador in a bull
ring. The two Crip Gang members duck the attempted blows
from the bumper jack.

The two Crip Gang Members at the same time try to subdue
Crazy James Eddie. Crip Gang Member #1 has a hold of the
bumper jack. Crip Gang Member #2 is able to punch Crazy
James Eddie several times.

This raises the ire of A.C., Lorenzo, Tam, Vince, and
Puddin'. They rush to the aid of Crazy James Eddie, by
pummeling the two Crip Gang Members.

> CRAZY JAMES EDDIE
> Fuck they ass up!

The fighting is fierce, the two Crip Gang Members don't go
down easy. Though outnumbered, the two Crip Gang Members
can't be overtaken. Theirs a pause in the fighting, everyone
is fatigued.

> TAM
> This shit ain't over.

> A.C.
> We gon' see you again nigga.

> CRIP GANG MEMBER #1
> Fuck the Piru Street Boys! This is
> Crip nigga.

Together, Crip Gang Member #1 and Crip Gang Member #2 trot
off. Crazy James Eddie rears back, bumper jack over his
head, and he chases after them.

> CRAZY JAMES EDDIE
> You mutha fucka's. Awwwwwwww!

The two Crip Gang Members pick up the pace leaving Crazy James Eddie, exhausted, holding the bumper jack.

INT. APARTMENT - BEDROOM - MORNING

Lying in the bed, A.C. is roused out of his sleep by a VOICE, his sister Erma.

                    ERMA (O.C.)
          A.C., get up! It's seven o'clock.

A.C. drags himself out of bed and wipes the sleep from his eyes. He grabs his pants from the closet, one leg goes in after the other.

Once dressed, he reaches into a dresser drawer. Inside are several RED DEVIL pills. A.C. picks one Red Devil up, pops it in his mouth, he swallows.

INT. APARTMENT - LIVING ROOM - MOMENTS LATER

A.C. walks in. Sitting on the couch, CIGARETTE hanging from her mouth, BEER in one hand is ERMA, an African American female 26.

                    ERMA
          Make sure you get to school on
          time.

                    A.C.
               (high)
          Yeah, I will.

Sluggish, A.C. walks out the door.

EXT. CENTENNIAL HIGH - CAMPUS - DAY

A.C. makes his way through students that are walking about. He runs into Lorenzo.

                    LORENZO
          Aye man, it's some dudes up here
          trippin'. You might know them.
          They say their Crips. One of them
          was at the fight when Ralph's nose
          got broken.

FLASHBACK:

EXT. COMPTON - RESIDENTIAL STREET - DAY

RALPH CARTER African American male 17, is fighting TOMMY
WAYNE African American male, 17. Ralph is getting the best
of Tommy. A BLACK MALE hands Tommy a SODA POP BOTTLE. Tommy
crowns Ralph across the nose, and blood gushes from his face.

END OF FLASHBACK:

EXT. CENTENNIAL HIGH - CAMPUS - DAY

A.C. is still standing with Lorenzo.

> A.C.
> Oh yeah. Where they at?

Rounding a building A.C. and Lorenzo stop. Strolling through
the quad is MARSHALL BENNETT African American male, 17.

> LORENZO
> That's one of the dudes right
> there.

> A.C.
> Is homeboy supposed to be a Crip?
> (yells)
> Aye homeboy, let me talk to you.

Marshall pauses, he looks in A.C.'s direction.

> A.C. (CONT'D)
> Come here.

A.C. and Lorenzo trot towards Marshall, he sprints off.
Marshall races over to a group of Crip Gang Members.
Marshall, animated, points at A.C. and Lorenzo as they're
getting closer.

A.C. and Lorenzo run up on the Crip Gang Members, stopping
abruptly. RICO African American male 17, steps out of the
crowd.

> RICO
> What's up cuz?

A.C. points at Marshall.

> A.C.
> I wanna talk to homeboy right
> there.

                    RICO
          Back off.

                    A.C.
          Who the hell are you?

                    RICO
          Rico, Crip, from Carver Park.

                    A.C.
          You're not a Crip. I'm a Crip.
             (looking around)
          I don't know any of you cats.

                    RICO
          We don't know you nigga. Now what?

                    A.C.
          Me and you head up.

A.C. and Rico square off. They fight hard until several Crip
Gang Members jump in. They swarm A.C., and Lorenzo jumps in
to help A.C., it's of little consequence.

Both A.C. and Lorenzo are beaten up and knocked to the
ground. Now in fetal positions, both A.C. and Lorenzo are
thoroughly kicked. Rico stands over them.

                    RICO
          Fuck with us again. You get the
          same treatment.

The Crip Gang Members walk off giving each other five.

EXT. PIRU STREET - HOUSE - DAY

MUSIC CUE: "Get Up, Get Into It, Get Involved" by James
Brown.

In the front yard, a rally is taking place. A contingent of
young adult male blacks is fired up. A.C. is animated, and
his emotions are running high.

                    A.C.
          We can't let outsiders run
          Centennial High School.

END MUSIC CUE:

Also present are Lorenzo, Tam, Lil Vince, Puddin, Crazy James
Eddie, and Ralph Carter, whose nose is bandaged

                         LORENZO
          These dudes say they Crips. They
          looking to jump on anybody that
          claims Piru Street Boys.

                         TAM
          They broke Ralph's nose. Jumped on
          A.C. and Lorenzo. We can't let
          them get away with that.

                         A.C.
          You older cats have to step up.
          Y'all went to Centennial. Crips
          are trying to take over Compton.

                         RALPH
          I see at least twenty five dudes
          out here. What y'all wanna do?

                         A.C.
          A lot of dudes out here in their
          twenties. I'm just fifteen. My
          homeboys, we all in high school.
          They call us the Piru street boys.
          Fuck that boy shit -- We the Piru
          street gang!

In unison, with angry expressions on their faces. Chants of
PIRU STREET GANG resound.

I/E. R.T.D. BUS - DAY

The BUS DRIVER pulls up to the BUS STOP, and the DOORS open.
Several PASSENGERS get off. Standing there is Raymond
Washington, he steps on board with a few CRIP GANG MEMBERS.
Raymond gives the Bus Driver a stern look.

                         RAYMOND
     Get up.

                         BUS DRIVER
     Huh?

                         RAYMOND
     I said get up.

                         BUS DRIVER
     I can't do that.

The Bus Driver is attacked, and this stuns the other
Passengers. They know better than to interfere. Raymond and
the Crip Gang Members throw the Bus Driver out the door.

He lands on the pavement at the feet of over a dozen Crip Gang Members. To the astonishment of the Passengers, the dozen or so Crip Gang Members are now on board.

                    RAYMOND
          Everybody stay <u>calm</u> and no one will
          get <u>hurt</u>.

Raymond jumps behind the wheel, puts it in gear, and pulls off.

Trailing the R.T.D. Bus is a caravan of five CARS, loaded with Gang Members.

EXT. CENTENNIAL HIGH - OFF CAMPUS - DAY

The R.T.D. Bus pulls up on a side street, and the doors open. Led by Raymond Washington, Crip Gang Members debark. Just then, the five carloads of Crip Gang Members pull up.

The car doors open, and Crip Gang Members pile out. Like insects, they scale the school fence.

EXT. CENTENNIAL HIGH - QUAD - DAY

Ralph, Lorenzo, Tam, Lil Vince, Puddin', and A.C. are standing around.

                    RALPH
          Check it out.

Raymond Washington is posted up in the lunch area. He is with a large contingent of Crip Gang Members.

                    TAM
          Let's go over there.

                    A.C.
          Hold up. I'll go talk to Raymond.

                    LIL VINCE
          You going over there by yourself?
          That ain't cool.

                    PUDDIN
          They gon' roll you up, man.

                    A.C.
          Nah, me and Raymond, we're cool. I
          was down with the Crips when I
          lived on the east side.

A.C. makes his way over to Raymond. As he gets closer,
Raymond notices A.C. and he walks toward him, meeting A.C.
halfway. They give each other the black handshake.

                    RAYMOND
          What's happenin' man?

                    A.C.
          What it be like.

                    RAYMOND
          Some of my homeboys havin' a
          problem up here. We gon' have to
          fuck some niggas up.

CRIP GANG MEMBER #3 whispers into Raymond's ear.

                    CRIP GANG MEMBER #3
          He's one of the Piru Street Boys.

Raymond looks confused.

                    RAYMOND
          You a Piru Street Boy? You down
          with the Crips, right?

                    A.C.
          Yeah, I'm down wit'em. And it's
          the Piru Street <u>gang</u>.

Raymond chuckles.

                    A.C. (CONT'D)
          I was jumped on by some dudes that
          say they Carver Park Crips. I
          didn't know any of them niggas.

                    RAYMOND
          I know'em, they Crips. Zane Smith,
          he on the football team, he's from
          Carver Park. Somebody broke into
          his locker, stole his leather
          jacket. On top of that, at a party
          on Piru Street. Some Carver Park
          Crips got jumped on and runoff. We
          here to settle the score.

                    A.C.
          Some dude name Tommy Wayne broke
          Ralph Carter's nose. Ralph is my
          cousin, I want you to help me get
          that dude.

                         RAYMOND
          I can't help you with Tommy, he's a
          Crip.

                         A.C.
          I hear you. Then let's make a
          truce between the Crips and Piru
          Street Gang.

                         RAYMOND
          Look man, me and you cool. But
          it's a Piru versus Crip thang.

INT. CENTENNIAL HIGH - CAFETERIA - DAY

Sitting at a table eating, we see several Piru Street Gang
members.

Lorenzo, CHARLES FISH FISHER, African American male 17, Tam,
Lil Vince, Ralph, WEASEL African American male 17, EDGAR
OWENS African American male 17, and JEROME BO ROME EDWARDS
African American male 17.

Raymond Washington along with a platoon of Crip Gang Members
walk in, they surround the table.

                         RAYMOND
          You cats the Piru Street Gang.

The Piru Street Gang quickly surveys the situation, they feel
the tension. Edgar Owens rises up from the table.

                         EDGAR OWENS
               (attitude)
          Yeah, why?

Raymond swiftly punches Edgar Owens knocking him out. The
Crips begin attacking all the Piru Street Gang Members,
overwhelming them.

Weasel and Jerome Bo Rome scatter. Tam, Lil Vince, and Ralph
are cornered. Charles Fish Fisher is courageously fighting
three Crips.

EXT. CENTENNIAL HIGH - QUAD - DAY

RALPH SUGERMAN NELSON African American male 17, is hanging
out with some Piru Street Gang Members. Weasel and Jerome Bo
Rome frantically come running up.

>   WEASEL
>   (winded)
>   Sugerman, the Crips up here.

>   JEROME BO ROME
>   They got the homies hemmed up in
>   the cafeteria.

Sugerman's senses heighten.

>   RALPH SUGERMAN NELSON
>   Let's go!

Sugerman takes off running, with Weasel and Jerome Bo Rome
right behind him, followed by several Piru Street gang
members.

INT. CENTENNIAL HIGH - CAFETERIA - DAY

A melee is underway, the Crips are dominating the fight.
They have the Piru Street Gang outnumbered when help arrives.
Sugerman, Weasel, Jerome Bo Rome, and a reserve of Piru
Street Gang members rush in to join the battle.

Momentum shifts when Sugerman pulls out a GUN. Pointing at
Crip Gang Members, he wheels it around with reckless abandon.

>   RALPH SUGERMAN NELSON
>   I'm fixing to kill all you niggas.

The Crips panic, including Raymond Washington, when they see
the gun.

>   RAYMOND
>   C'mon, let's go!

All the Crips retreat, running out the door.

>   RALPH SUGERMAN NELSON
>   Go get their ass!

The remaining Piru Street Gang Members make chase.

MONTAGE.

EXT. CENTENNIAL HIGH - CAMPUS - DAY

Running for their lives, Crips are chased by Piru Street Gang
Members.

Six Crip Gang Members barely escape the grasp of Piru Street Gang Members by hopping the fence.

Piru Street Gang Members tackle two Crips, they deliver a beatdown.

A Crip Gang Member is curled up on the ground, he's being stomped and kicked by Piru Street Gang Members.

Trapped amongst the BUNGALOWS, nowhere to hide. Three Crips are slowly approached by a horde of Piru Street Gang Members. They are engulfed by the gang and beaten severely.

END OF MONTAGE.

EXT. LORENZO'S HOUSE - DAY

Hanging out on the porch. An intense debate is going on between Lorenzo, Puddin', and MONROE SOCKEYE COOPER, an African American male, 20.

                    LORENZO
          Them mutha fucka's invaded the
          school like an army.

                    PUDDIN
          They had us surrounded in the
          cafeteria. Raymond knocked out
          Edgar.

                    LORENZO
          We were throwin' down, then
          Sugerman rushed in. He pulled out
          a gun, the Crips cheese'd up when
          they saw the gun. They hauled ass
          out the Cafeteria.

                    SOCKEYE
          Dig this... I know Raymond. I was
          down with the Avenues on the east
          side. The Crips are getting bigger
          and bigger. They wanna take over
          every neighborhood. Right now they
          got Compton.

                    LORENZO
          There's a dance tonight at Gonzales
          Park. I heard Raymond is gon' be
          there.

                    PUDDIN
          I ain't having it. The Crips at
          Gonzales Park. That's our
          backyard, <u>fuck</u> <u>that</u>.

                    SOCKEYE
          Check it out. I'm down with y'all.
          I'll lead the Piru's in a fight
          against the Crips. Let all yo
          homeboys know. Bring knives,
          pipes, and chains. Whatever y'all
          can get your hands on.

EXT. GONZALES PARK - PARKING LOT - NIGHT

With a Gangster stroll, the Piru Street Gang makes its
entrance.

Lorenzo, Sugerman, Bo Rome, NARDY African American male 17,
DARRYL JOHNSON African American male 17, A.C., Puddin', Tam,
Lil Vince, Ralph, Fish, Sockeye, and Weasel announce their
presents.

                    DARRYL JOHNSON
          Piiiii-ru!

                    NARDY
          Piiiii-ru!

Five members of the Crip gang, wearing ACE DUCE hats, are
hanging out when they are spotted by the Piru Street Gang.

                    FISH
          Looks like some Crips right there.

                    RALPH SUGERMAN NELSON
          Let's go kick their ass.

Sugerman breaks into a sprint. Lorenzo, Bo Rome, Nardy,
Darryl Johnson, A.C., Puddin', Tam, Lil Vince, Ralph, Fish,
Sockeye, and Weasel take off right behind him.

The five Crip Gang Members are completely caught off guard.
They are under assault by the Piru Street Gang.

The Crip Gang Members fight back gallantly, and suddenly they
retreat, running toward the GYMNASIUM.

MUSIC CUE: "Slippin' Into Darkness" by War.

INT. GONZALES PARK - GYMNASIUM - DAY

The dance floor is filled with teens and young adults. Five
members of the Crip gang enter, looking exhausted as they
gather themselves. Taking a moment to survey the crowd, they
start to perform a distinctive chirp whistle with their
fingers. Throughout the dance, other Crip gang members
respond to the sound. Like a homing signal, they begin to
make their way toward the source of the whistle.

END MUSIC CUE:

EXT. GONZALEZ PARK - GYMNASIUM - DAY

Sugerman, Lorenzo, Bo Rome, Nardy, Darryl Johnson, A.C.,
Puddin', Tam, Lil Vince, Ralph, Fish, Sockeye, and Weasel try
to storm the front entrance.

They are quickly confronted at the door by STAFF EMPLOYEE #1
and four SECURITY GUARDS.

                    STAFF EMPLOYEE #1
          Hold it, hold it, hold it.

                    RALPH SUGERMAN NELSON
          We want to go in.

 Staff Employee #1 looks at the gang members suspiciously.

                    STAFF EMPLOYEE #1
          You can't go in.

                    A.C.
          What do you mean? I have my money
          right here.

A.C. holds up three one-dollar bills.

                    STAFF EMPLOYEE #1
          None of you guys are gettin' in.

                    LIL VINCE
          That's bullshit man.

Lil Vince watches four teens enter the dance.

                    LIL VINCE (CONT'D)
          How are you gon' let them in and
          not let us in?

                    STAFF EMPLOYEE #1
          Forget it. You guys ain't gettin'
          in the dance.

Lil Vince steps to Staff Employee #1.

                    LIL VINCE
          I ought'a...

The four Security Guards step toward Lil Vince ready for
action. Lil Vince is reluctant to back down. The rest of
the Piru Gang takes a defensive posture. Things are tense,
Sockeye grabs Lil Vince by the arm.

                    SOCKEYE
          C'mon, let's go. Our fight ain't
          with them. We got other business.

The Piru Street Gang Members compose themselves and walk off.

Sockeye leads them to a door in the back. The low tone of
MUSIC can be heard coming from inside the gymnasium.

Sockeye takes a CLAW HAMMER, he strikes the DOORKNOB with
fury. The Piru Street Gang just watches, as Sockeye, with
all his might tries to rip the HINGES off. To no avail,
Sockeye tries the pry the door open.

                    LIL VINCE
          Save that energy for the Crips.

A VOICE looms from the shadows. This is Crip Gang Member #4.

                    CRIP GANG MEMBER #4 (O.C.)
          You looking for us?

Stepping out of the Shadows is 50 CRIP GANG MEMBERS.

                    A.C.
          Aw shit.

The Crips mount a mass attack, they charge the Piru Street
Gang. Having no chance, Sugerman, Lorenzo, Bo Rome, Nardy,
Darryl Johnson, A.C., Puddin', Tam, Vince, Ralph, Fish,
Sockeye, and Weasel are chased into the darkness.

EXT. CORNER OF PIRU STREET AND CENTRAL AVENUE - NIGHT

The Crips, led by Raymond Washington, have gathered a group
of approximately 100 gang members. They make their way down
Piru Street, concealing themselves between various
residential homes.

Sugerman, Lorenzo, Bo Rome, Nardy, Darryl Johnson, A.C.,
Puddin', Tam, Lil Vince, Ralph, Fish, Sockeye, and Weasel are
on watch.

Suddenly Sockeye comes out of hiding. He runs into the
middle of the street with an AFRICAN SPEAR in his hand.

                    SOCKEYE
          Hold up, I'm Sockeye, I was down
          with the Avenues. Now I'm down
          with the Piru Street Gang. I'm
          calling out Raymond Washington to a
          head-up fight!

In between one of the Residential Homes. We see Sugerman and
Lorenzo preparing to light a MOLOTOV COCKTAIL.

Raymond Washington steps through the crowd of Crips. He
pulls out a gun and begins shooting. Sockeye dodges bullets
as they barely miss him, ricocheting off a car and skirting
the ground.

The sound of GUNSHOTS can be heard as Bo Rome and Nardy light
their Molotov Cocktail. They run into the middle of the
street tossing the Molotov Cocktail. It lands next to some
Crips bursting into flames.

Just then, Lorenzo, Darryl Johnson, A.C., Puddin', Tam, Lil
Vince, Ralph, Fish, and Weasel come out from hiding.

They all began lobbing Molotov Cocktails at the Crip Gang
Members. Like grenades, the Molotov Cocktails hit the ground
exploding into flames.

The Crips take off running barely escaping injury. With the
African Spear in hand, Sockeye give chase after the Crips.

                    SOCKEYE (CONT'D)
               (shouting)
          What you running for, got damn
          cowards.

Sockeye launches the African Spear like a javelin. It caroms
off the pavement just missing a Crip Gang Member.

EXT. CENTENNIAL HIGH - CAMPUS - DAY

Close on school BELL RINGING. The bustle of STUDENTS walking
the HALLWAYS ducking into classrooms.

INT. CENTENNIAL HIGH - GYMNASIUM - DAY

Close on MR. MCCRUMBY, male African American 40s, looking
intensely serious. Sitting in the bleachers to the left of
McCrumby are Crip Gang members.

Zane Smith, ZACHARY SMITH male African American 16, FELTON
male African American 17, JOE GLUE BABY BARNELL male African
American 17, BABY RONNIE male African American 17, Rico, ROY
TUCKER male African American 17, BLACK JOHNNY male African
American 16, TIM NELSON male African American 17, ROBERT
COLOR BAR BENFORD male African American 16, CRIP AL male
African American 17, and Marshall Bennett.

Sitting to Mr. McCrumby's right are Piru Street Gang Members
Lorenzo, Tam, Lil Vince, Puddin', Sugerman, and Ralph Carter.

                    MR. MCCRUMBY
          This is a School, a place of
          education -- not the wild west.
          You guys want to fight and kill
          each other. Fine -- kill each
          other. But not here -- not at
          Centennial High School.

                    LORENZO
          Mr. McCrumby. The Crips are trying
          to take over the School. We not
          gon' let that happen.

                    MR. MCCRUMBY
          The Crips. The <u>Piru</u> <u>Street</u> <u>Boys</u>.

                    TAM
          Gang. The Piru Street Gang.

                    MR. MCCRUMBY
          Boys. Gang. I don't give a damn
          what you cats call yourself. Just
          a bunch of idiots, that's what you
          are. We're not even ten years
          removed from the Watts riots.
          Blacks revolting against Police
          brutality. Social injustice, the
          world was watching. You guys do
          the Black Panthers a disservice.
          Huey Newton, Bobby Seale, Elbert
          Howard... They would be ashamed of
          you cats.

The DOOR opens, and Mr. McCrumby holds his peace. Everyone's
attention shifts to the figure standing in the doorway.

This is MR. WENDELL H PAGE, male African American, 40s. He
walks in, stands next to Mr. McCrumby, and shakes his hand.
Mr. Page then faces the gang members sitting in the
bleachers.

> WENDELL H PAGE
> For those of you that don't know
> me. I'm Principle Wendell Page.
> You all know Mr. McCrumby. Many of
> you have taken his Physical
> education class.

Mr. Page begins to pace back and forth.

> WENDELL H PAGE (CONT'D)
> It was Mr. McCrumby's suggestion
> that this gang summit be held. I
> thought to myself. I will not
> concede to the whims of a bunch of
> teenage hoodlums. I became very
> angry. But it's my job, Mr.
> McCrumby's job, as educators to
> help every student. Not just the
> student that excels in school, but
> the student that is failing. That
> failing student is inherently more
> important to redeem than the
> student that does well in school.
> As I look at you young black men.
> I can't help but see failed
> opportunity, wasted potential. I
> have looked at the school records
> of every student sitting in these
> bleachers. You call yourselves
> gang members, I call you students.
> While you're on this campus, that's
> exactly what you are, students.
> The fighting between Crips and Piru
> Street Boys...

Tam is about to interject, Lorenzo grabs his shoulder pulling
him back.

> WENDELL H PAGE (CONT'D)
> ...is disrupting school functions.
>   (exclaim)
> This has to stop. A lot of the
> young men here played youth sports
> together, partied together. Now
> you're at each other's throats. I
> implore, I demand, that both gangs
> call a truce on campus. I want the
> truce to extend off-campus as well.

There is a brief silence. The Crips look dumbfounded, so do
the Piru Street Gang members. Both gangs whisper amongst
each other.

> ZANE
> We'll agree to a truce if they
> will.

Still, another pause amongst everyone.

> LORENZO
> Alright, let's agree. But we can't
> promise the truce will go beyond
> the campus.

Mr. Page and Mr. McCrumby both have the look of exasperation.

INT. LOS ANGELES POLICE STATION - SQUAD ROOM - DAY

On the wall we see, 77th Street Division, "To Protect and to
Serve." The camera pulls back, revealing a uniform Officer.
ROBERT MICHAEL, white male 30s, stands before a room full of
UNIFORMED COPS.

> ROBERT MICHAEL
> Most of you know me, for those who
> don't. I am Sergeant Robert
> Michael. I have been ordered to
> set up a gang Intelligence Unit.
> I'm looking for volunteers. This
> unit has been given the acronym of
> TRASH, or Total Resources Against
> Street Hoodlums, headed by Sergeant
> Beno Hernandez.

BENO HERNANDEZ, a Latino male in his 30s, is sitting amongst
the uniformed cops. Beno acknowledges everyone with a hand
gesture.

> ROBERT MICHAEL (CONT'D)
> Officer Hernandez and I will work
> in tandem to coordinate this
> effort. Gangs in Los Angeles are
> nothing new. However, in recent
> years, a new black gang has sprung
> up. They are plaguing South Los
> Angeles and its surrounding cities.
> Crime has risen in these
> communities, schools have become
> breeding grounds for gang
> recruitment. We have to put a stop
> to it. One gang, in particular, is
> on our radar. They call themselves
> the Crips, are a scourge.
> Residents are up in arms and in
> complete fear. So they look to us.

Sergeant Michael points to a police motto on the wall.

                    ROBERT MICHAEL (CONT'D)
          You see what that says? "To
          Protect and to Serve." Anyone that
          wants to join the gang unit, see me
          in my office tomorrow. Sergeant
          Hernandez, I'd like to have a word
          with you. Everyone else is
          dismissed.

The room clears of uniformed cops. Beno walks up to Robert
Michael.

                    BENO HERNANDEZ
          Nice introduction.

                    ROBERT MICHAEL
          I don't think we'll have a problem
          with guys volunteering.

                    BENO HERNANDEZ
          Nah, we won't.

                    ROBERT MICHAEL
          The Crips are out of control.
          We're going to have to kick some
          ass. Everything will not be by the
          book. You on board with that?

                    BENO HERNANDEZ
          Whatever it takes. I'm ready.

                    ROBERT MICHAEL
          Good.

INT. HOME OF VIOLET SAMUEL - GARAGE - DAY

Cheeks puffed out like a blowfish, Tookie feverishly bench
presses 250 lbs. Raymond Washington, exerting himself, curls
dumbbells in both hands...

                    RAYMOND
          Word is, the Pirus want a truce.

Tookie lets the barbell come to rest on the barbell Rack.
Arms bulging, Tookie sits up on the end of the bench.

                    TOOKIE
          Fuck a truce. It's Crip or get
          rolled over.

Raymond Washington sits the dumbbells on the Floor.

                    RAYMOND
          A.C. can help with the Pirus. The
          Brims are a problem too. Big
          Country don't want the Brims to
          join the Crips.

Sitting in the corner, Craig Craddock cleans his PISTOL.

                    CRAIG
          Let me deal with Big Country.

INT. CENTENNIAL HIGH - PRINCIPAL WENDELL PAGE'S OFFICE - DAY

On his desk is a PLAQUE that says, Principal Wendell Page.
Seated behind the desk looking a bit irritated is Mr. Page.

Standing before him are two uniformed Compton Police
Officers. ARTHUR TAYLOR, male African American 30s, and
SHIRLEY LIDGE, female African American 30s.

                    OFFICER LIDGE
          You have a gang problem on this
          campus. Protecting thugs won't
          help the situation.

                    WENDELL H PAGE
          I resent that assumption.

                    OFFICER TAYLOR
          I understand you have a way of
          dealing with delinquent students.
          The gang members at this school are
          predators.

The BUZZER on the Desk Phone goes off. Mr. Page picks up the
RECEIVER.

                    WENDELL H PAGE
          Yes. Send him in, please.

The DOOR opens and in walks Mr. McCrumby.

                    WENDELL H PAGE (CONT'D)
          Mr. McCrumby. This is Officer
          Lidge and Officer Taylor of the
          Compton P.D. Mr. McCrumby is a
          Physical Education teacher here at
          the school.
                    (to Mr. McCrumby)
          I informed them about the meeting
          between the Crips and the Piru
          Street Gang.

                    OFFICER TAYLOR
          Who's idea was it to organize the
          gang meeting?

                    MR. MCCRUMBY
          It was mine. I felt It was the
          best way to initiate a truce
          between the gangs. To ease
          tensions on campus.

                    OFFICER LIDGE
          Mr. McCrumby, you are a gym
          teacher. Not a gang mediator.

                    OFFICER TAYLOR
          You may have been well-intended.
          That was a bad idea. Now you've
          opened the school up for lawsuits,
          you can lose your job. You can be
          held liable too Mr. Page.

                    OFFICER LIDGE
          We want the names of the gang
          members that were at this meeting.

Both Mr. Page and Mr. McCrumby look very worried.

EXT. GONZALEZ PARK - EVENING

Agitated, the Piru Street Gang has amassed. A.C., Tam,
Puddin', Lil Vince, Ralph Carter, Sockeye, and Sugerman are
in the midst of the contentious group.

                    LORENZO
          We agreed to a truce.

MCKINNEY OWENS, male African American 18, and TERRY CARTER,
male African American 16 are visibly upset.

                    MCKINNEY OWENS
          Nobody talked to me. Cuz some
          teacher said we should make a truce
          with the Crips, you agreed?

                    TERRY CARTER
          They broke my brother, Ralph's nose
          with a bottle. I'm supposed to
          forget that.

                    LIL VINCE
          McKinney, you're my older brother --
          You weren't at the meeting. We had
          to make a decision.

> A.C.
> Ralph, Terry. We cousins, I'm down
> with y'all. I know Raymond, I was
> a Crip, I'll talk to him. Let's
> give the truce a chance.

Grumbling and moans are heard amongst the gang.

> PUDDIN
> I was at the meeting. Some of them
> dudes were our homeboys.

> RALPH SUGERMAN NELSON
> Fuck it. Roll with the truce. If
> it don't work. Let the Crips be
> the ones that break it.

A Compton Police Squad CAR rolls into the parking lot. It
rolls straight up to the gang members.

> LIL VINCE
> The cops.

Most of the Piru Street Gang members scatter. A.C.,
Sugerman, and Ralph hold their ground. Officers Lidge and
Taylor quickly exit the squad car.

> OFFICER TAYLOR
> OK, hold it right there.

Officer Lidge draws her GUN.

> OFFICER LIDGE
> On the ground, now.

Officer Taylor searches A.C., Sugerman, and Ralph. He finds
nothing.

> OFFICER TAYLOR
> Alright, where's the gun?

> PUDDIN
> What are you talkin' bout? Ain't
> nobody got a gun.

> A.C.
> You trippin'. We ain't did
> nothing.

Officer Taylor cuffs A.C.

> RALPH SUGERMAN NELSON
> Man, what you doin'?

                         OFFICER TAYLOR
              What I'm doing?

Officer Taylor takes Sugerman to the ground and cuffs him.

                         RALPH SUGERMAN NELSON
              Aye man, you violatin' my rights.

Officer Taylor picks Sugerman up off the ground.

                         OFFICER TAYLOR
              Oh yeah. You have the right to
              remain silent. Anything you say
              can and will be used against you.

A.C., Sugerman, and Ralph are stuffed into the back of the
police car.

EXT. COMPTON POLICE DEPARTMENT - NIGHT

Establishing shot of the BUILDING MARQUEE.

INT. COMPTON POLICE DEPARTMENT - INTERROGATION ROOM - NIGHT

The room is dimly lit. A SPOTLIGHT shines in the face of
A.C., as he is pressed by DETECTIVE #3, male white 30s, and
DETECTIVE #4, male white 30s.

                         DETECTIVE #3
              Who's the leader of the gang?

                         A.C.
              What gang?

                         DETECTIVE #4
              You know what gang. Don't play
              dumb got damn it.

                         DETECTIVE #3
              There was a gang fight on Piru
              Street. Gunshots were fired. Who
              was it?

                         A.C.
              I don't know what you talkin' bout.

Detective #3 grabs A.C. by his collar pulling him out of the
chair.

                         DETECTIVE #3
              Who was doing the shooting?

                         A.C.
          I wasn't at no gang fight. I'm
          telling you, I don't know what you
          talkin' bout.

Detective #3 pushes A.C. back down into the chair. Detective
#4 gets in his face.

                         DETECTIVE #4
          You were throwing cocktails,
          weren't you?

                         A.C.
          I don't drink.

Detective #4 abruptly slaps A.C. upside his head.

                         DETECTIVE #3
          That's enough. We're not going to
          get anything out of him.

INT. COMPTON POLICE DEPARTMENT - HOLDING CELL - DAY

The BARS open, and the JAILER pushes A.C. in. Looking
disheveled, A.C. is greeted by Sugerman and Ralph.

                         RALPH SUGERMAN NELSON
          You alright?

                         RALPH
          We got the same treatment, slapped
          around.

                         A.C.
          They pissed cuz I didn't break.

A.C. rubs his sore cheek. He looks at the floor and is
captivated by some graffiti, a name that says "BOBALOUIE."

                         A.C. (CONT'D)
          That's what I'm gon' call myself.

                         RALPH SUGERMAN NELSON
          What?

A.C. points to the graffiti name on the floor.

                         RALPH
          Bobalouie?

                         A.C.
          Yeah, Bobalouie -- King Bobalouie.

INT. WASHINGTON HIGH SCHOOL - CLASSROOM - DAY

Sitting in the rear of the class is SHERYL, a female African
American 17, behind her sits Bonnie Quarles. It appears that
they are whispering to one another. Sitting across from
Bonnie is Tookie, he is eavesdropping on Sheryl and Bonnie.

                    BONNIE
          What'd she say?

                    SHERYL
          Talkin' shit about I want her dude.
          She wants to fight me.

                    BONNIE
          She gon' get her ass kicked. I got
          your back girl.

Tookie leans over and interjects.

                    TOOKIE
               (whisper)
          You ain't fighting nobody.

                    BONNIE
          Boy, mind your business.

TEACHER #3 is writing on the CHALKBOARD. She turns around to
see Sheryl, Bonnie, and Tookie's heads joined together like
triplets. Teacher #3 quickly walks over to the three.

                    TEACHER #3
          Excuse me. I don't mean to
          interrupt. It's class time, not
          lunchtime. Bonnie, I allow you to
          hang out in my classroom, while you
          ditch the class you should be
          attending. Please show the other
          students some consideration.

                    BONNIE
          I'm sorry.

                    TEACHER #3
          That goes for you too, Stanley and
          Sheryl.

Just then the BELL RINGS.

EXT. WASHINGTON HIGH SCHOOL - QUAD AREA - DAY

A group of African American female teens is huddled together.
Sheryl, Bonnie, BAD BESSIE 17, BLACK CONNIE 16, PRETTY CONNIE
15, GOLDIE 17, BIG PAM 17, COOKIE 16, and PRETTY ROBIN 17.

                    BONNIE
          Let's find that bitch and fuck her
          up!

                    BAD BESSIE
          I know where she is.

INT. WASHINGTON HIGH SCHOOL - BATHROOM - DAY

FEMALE #1, 17, and FEMALE #2, 17 are prancing in the mirror.

                    FEMALE #1
          I don't know who that bitch thinks
          she fuckin' with.

The DOOR opens. Sheryl, Bonnie, Bad Bessie, Black Connie,
Pretty Connie, Goldie, Big Pam, Cookie, and Pretty Robin all
file in. Sheryl directs her attention to Female #1.

                    SHERYL
          What now bitch! You still want to
          get down?

                    FEMALE #1
          Fuck all you bitches. We suppose
          to be scared?

                    BONNIE
          Bitch we Criplettes. You bout to
          get beat the fuck up!

Female #1 pulls out a KNIFE. BONNIE in turn pulls out a 25
CALIBER PISTOL. Female #1 is not daunted.

                    FEMALE #1
          So what? You gon' shoot me?

                    BONNIE
          Nah bitch, you gon' fight Sheryl.
          Put the knife up, or you gon' get
          shot.

Female #1 gives the knife to Female #2. Sheryl rushes Female
#1, the fighting is fierce. Bonnie hands the 25 Caliber
Pistol to Bad Bessie.

                    BONNIE (CONT'D)
          Watch that bitch with the knife.

Bad Bessie gives Female #2 a mean look, then trains the 25
Caliber Pistol on her. Bonnie jumps in the fight, helping
Sheryl, Female #1 is beaten bloody.

EXT. BONNIE QUARLES HOUSE - BACKYARD - EVENING

Tookie strolls in. Bonnie is smoking a MARIJUANA JOINT. She
blows the SMOKE from her mouth, then passes the joint to
Sheryl.

                    TOOKIE
          I'm hearing shit around school bout
          a girl's gang. They call
          themselves the Criplettes.

                    BONNIE
               (cool)
          Is that right?

Sheryl takes a drag from the joint.

                    TOOKIE
          What you tryin' to do. You
          trippin', starting a gang.

                    BONNIE
          You in a gang. Don't try to tell
          me I can't be in one.

                    SHERYL
          We have to deal with bitches that
          want to start shit. We can't be
          running to you and yo homeboys.

                    TOOKIE
          The Criplettes -- Really?

                    BONNIE
          Yeah, the Criplettes, and bitches
          better not fuck with us.

EXT. THE LOS ANGELES TIMES - DAY

Establishing shot of the BUILDING and MARQUEE.

INT. THE LOS ANGELES TIMES - OFFICE - DAY

Bustling with activity, we see a DOOR, stenciled on the
FROSTED GLASS WINDOW is EDITOR Bill Thomas. Briskly walking,
JERRY COHEN 49, male white, opens the door and walks in.
Sitting behind his desk looking extremely busy is BILL THOMAS
47, male white.

                    JERRY COHEN
               Bill, I want to do an in-depth
               article on gangs.

Looking down at the materials on his desk.

                    BILL THOMAS
               Jerry, I have deadlines to meet.
               That's just recycled news. What's
               original about that story?

                    JERRY COHEN
               I want to focus on a particular
               gang -- a black gang.

                    BILL THOMAS
                    (dismissive)
               Sounds like a waste of copy.

                    JERRY COHEN
               Have you ever heard of the Crips?

                    BILL THOMAS
               No, but I'm sure you'll fill me in.

                    JERRY COHEN
               They're a juvenile gang that's been
               plaguing the South Los Angeles
               community. LAPD has assembled a
               task force specifically to deal
               with the Crips.

                    BILL THOMAS
               Really. Now I'm interested -- run
               with it.

Jerry is all smiles.

INT. LOS ANGELES POLICE STATION - OFFICE - DAY

CAPTAIN BARS stands out on his COLLAR. Officer MARVIN P.
KING, a male white 40s, places a folder in his file cabinet.

                         MARVIN P. KING
          There is concern in all law
          enforcement. We're all aware of
          group activity. But how much group
          activity by black youth is lawless,
          and how much of that which is
          lawless, actually is the work of
          gangs?

Notepad in hand, Jerry Cohen is sitting in a chair. Marvin
P. King takes a seat behind his desk.

                         JERRY COHEN
          There has been a reemergence of
          juvenile gangs in South Los
          Angeles. Of which the Crips are
          best known and many say the most
          notorious.

Jerry puts on his glasses, he refers to his notes.

                         JERRY COHEN (CONT'D)
          The following is a conversation
          that occurred between a seventy-
          seventh street division Los Angeles
          police officer and a black youth he
          arrested. "Are you a Crip?" The
          patrolman asked. "Yeah, man, I'm a
          Crip." "What's a Crip?" "I don't
          know."
                    (looking up)
          "We've had to contend with this for
          years."

EXT. LOS ANGELES POLICE STATION - PARKING LOT - DAY

LAPD squad cars are parked in stalls. A white MALE OFFICER
retrieves his SHOTGUN from a squad CAR. He and Jerry,
PENCIL, and NOTEPAD in hand, begin to walk. Jerry listens
intently and takes meticulous notes.

                         MALE OFFICER
          Most of it's a lot of talk. Even
          though juvenile crime is much the
          same as always, people are uptight,
          blowing the situation out of
          proportion. Not just uptight about
          crime, but uptight about the
          failure of remedial programs down
          here, uptight about the economy.

INT. LOS ANGELES SHERIFF'S DEPARTMENT - HALLWAY - DAY

UNIFORMED OFFICERS are walking to and fro. SERGEANTS STRIPES
on his sleeves, a somewhat animated Officer RAY MORRIS, white
male 40s, walks with Jerry.

                    RAY MORRIS
          We aren't seeing the gang concept
          in the old sense. We are seeing a
          new type of gang that bands
          together at certain times.

                    JERRY COHEN
          How is the Sheriff's Department
          dealing with the juvenile gang
          known as the Crips?

                    RAY MORRIS
          Gangs are here one day, then we
          don't hear of them anymore. It
          varies from week to week. We can't
          tell how many Crips there are.

EXT. SOUTH LOS ANGELES - SURFACE STREETS - DAY

In his car, Jerry slowly drives by BUILDINGS that have
GRAFFITI written on them. Among the defaced properties, we
see the words "Crip Here!"

EXT. RESIDENTIAL STREET - APARTMENT BUILDING - DAY

Standing with a NOTEPAD, and PENCIL in hand. Jerry is with a
group of five black male teens. They are CRIP GANG MEMBER
#5, CRIP GANG MEMBER #6, CRIP GANG MEMBER #7, CRIP GANG
MEMBER #8, and CRIP GANG MEMBER #9.

                    CRIP GANG MEMBER #5
          I know adults, police -- the
          community is concerned about us.

                    CRIP GANG MEMBER #6
          The shit is unfair. We get blamed
          for shit we ain't even do.

                    CRIP GANG MEMBER #7
          Yeah, like that white dude that got
          killed on Figueroa Street. The
          paper said fifteen kids, boys, and
          girls, ten to seventeen years old
          beat'em to death. They blamed that
          on the Crips.

                    CRIP GANG MEMBER #8
Man, we do our thang. But not no
shit like that.

                    JERRY COHEN
Who started the Crips? How did
they originate?

                    CRIP GANG MEMBER #9
I'm not sure, some guys on the east
side formed the gang to protect
they selves against another gang
called the Avenues.

                    JERRY COHEN
The concept of the name. What's
the meaning behind the word Crip?

                    CRIP GANG MEMBER #9
I'm not sure about that either.

                    CRIP GANG MEMBER #5
I heard it came from the name
"cripple," because of the way the
gang members walked with canes.

Jerry notices the way the teens are dressed, waistline
leather coats, cuffed Levi's, biscuit shoes, ace duce hats,
earrings in the left ear lobe.

                    JERRY COHEN
Your clothing, style of dress. Is
that a trademark of the Crips?

                    CRIP GANG MEMBER #6
Yeah, man. It lets people know,
don't fuck with us.

                    JERRY COHEN
Why do youths become Crips, for
that matter -- even join a gang?

                    CRIP GANG MEMBER #6
It's sticking together. It's being
together with brothers. It's a
brotherhood, toughness. Like back
when there was slavery, they always
were trying to separate us.

                    CRIP GANG MEMBER #7
Aye, man. Is this really gon' be
in the paper?

                    JERRY COHEN
         Sure is, the L.A. Times.

INT. HOME OF BOB CREAR - NIGHT

Dressed in cool knit pants, flashy polyester shirt, and knit
sport coat. 6 foot 4 inches, 240 pound African-American BOB
BIG HAWK CREAR is on his way out the door. He is stopped by
his mother, MRS. CREAR 40s, female African American.

                    MRS. CREAR
         Don't go up there. You know how
         they get to actin'. You might get
         into some trouble.

                    BOB BIG HAWK CREAR
         Mama, I'm not gon' do anything
         wrong. I have money, I just wanna
         check out the show. Plus, I've
         never been to the Palladium.

EXT. HOME OF BOB CREAR - CONTINUOUS

Bob comes out the front door gets into his 1962 Chevy Impala
Super Sport and drives off.

I/E. 1965 RAMBLER - NIGHT

MUSIC CUE: "Superfly" by Curtis Mayfield.

JUDSON BACOT 22, male African American, and James Cuzz
Cunningham are driving north on Western Avenue. Judson
checks his SMITH & WESSON 22 CALIBER PISTOL.

Cuzz, behind the wheel, makes a left turn at the intersection
of SUNSET & WESTERN AVE. Now headed east on Sunset Blvd they
approach the PALLADIUM.

The MARQUEE on the building says *Soul Train Presents Curtis
Mayfield, Wilson Pickett, and War*. They park on a side
street just north of Sunset Blvd.

END MUSIC CUE:

Judson and Cuzz get out of the car, they walk toward the
Palladium. As they walk along Judson and Cuzz spot WHITE GUY
#1 strolling with two white friends.

                    JUDSON
         Check it out.

                    JAMES CUZZ CUNNINGHAM
          Yeah.

                         JUDSON
                    (shouts)
          Aye, I need to ask y'all something.

That gets their attention. White Guy #1 and his two white
friends stop. Judson and Cuzz walk right up to them.

                    WHITE GUY #1
          What's happening?

                    JUDSON
          You guys going to the concert?

                    WHITE GUY #1
          Yeah, we are.

Judson pulls out his Smith & Wesson 22 Caliber pistol.

                    JUDSON
          This is a robbery, don't make it a
          murder.

                                        SMASH CUT TO:

Judson and Cuzz are now robbing several BLACK GUYS. Judson
with his Smith & Wesson 22 Caliber pistol trained on the
Black Guys.

                    JUDSON (CONT'D)
          This is a two-eleven, don't make it
          a one-eighty-seven.

Some PEDESTRIANS happen on to the robbery in progress.

                    JAMES CUZZ CUNNINGHAM
          Mind your business and keep moving.

The Pedestrians, with sheepish looks on their faces, do just
that and keep walking.

EXT. HOLLYWOOD PALLADIUM - NIGHT

Bob Big Hawk Crear is with CRIP GANG MEMBER #10 and CRIP GANG
MEMBER #11. They walk to the ticket window. Bob overhears
CONCERT GOER #1, CONCERT GOER #2, and CONCERT GOER #3

                    CONCERT GOER #1
          I thought you had some money.

                    CONCERT GOER #2
          Nah, I told you I didn't.

                    CONCERT GOER #3
          I got my ten dollars to get in.
          What y'all thought this was a free
          concert?

Bob steps up to them.

                    BOB BIG HAWK CREAR
          You guys wanna get in to see the
          concert?

The Concert Goers look puzzled.

                    CONCERT GOER #1
          Yeah.

                    BOB BIG HAWK CREAR
          Follow me.

With a gangsta stride, Bob starts walking. The Concert Goers
hesitate for a second. Then like baby ducks that follow
their mother. Concert Goer #1, Concert Goer #2, and Concert
Goer #3 quickly follow Bob.

                    CRIP GANG MEMBER #10
          Aye Big Hawk cuz, where you going?

                    CRIP GANG MEMBER #11
          You trippin' cuz. We ain't got
          time for this.

Flustered looks on their faces, Crip Gang Member #10 and Crip
Gang Member #11 hustle to catch up with Bob.

                                        SMASH CUT TO:

The low tone of MUSIC is heard from a REAR DOOR behind the
venue. Bob Big Hawk Crear, Concert Goer #1, Concert Goer #2,
Concert Goer #3, Crip Gang Member #10, and Crip Gang Member
#11 approach the rear door.

                    CRIP GANG MEMBER #10
          Cuz, what are you doin'?

Bob puts his EAR on the rear door.

                    CRIP GANG MEMBER #11
          C'mon man, let's get the fuck outta
          here.

                    BOB BIG HAWK CREAR
          Stand back.

Bob, with one thunderous kick, BAM! The rear door flies
open.

MUSIC CUE: "The Cisco Kid" by War.

                    BOB BIG HAWK CREAR (CONT'D)
          Y'all go on in.

                    CONCERT GOER #1
          No Shit!

                    CONCERT GOER #2
          Right on man!

                    CONCERT GOER #3
          You are one righteous dude!

Concert Goer #1, Concert Goer #2, and Concert Goer #3 strut
through the rear door.

END MUSIC CUE:

I/E. ARBY'S RESTAURANT - NIGHT

Judson Bacot and James Cuzz Cunningham are eating roast beef
sandwiches. They wipe their faces, take the last sip of soda
pop and walk outside.

Judson and Cuzz standing out front, check out the scene.

                    JUDSON
          Looks like the concert is over.

Across the street, people are filing out of the Palladium.

CHARLES ALEXANDER FOSTER, a male African American 17, is
wearing a long, black leather Maxi coat. He is with ROBERT
BROOKS BALLOU JR., a male African American 16. They are
walking across Sunset Blvd when Judson spots the two.

                    JUDSON (CONT'D)
          C'mon.

Judson and Cuzz trot across Sunset Blvd. They are now about
20 feet away from Charles Alexander Foster and Robert Brooks
Ballou Jr.

                    JUDSON (CONT'D)
          Hey dude, hey dude!

Charles stops, he turns around, and Robert Brooks Ballou Jr., unaware continues walking.

                    CHARLES ALEXANDER
          Me?

Cuzz is in lockstep with Judson, and they confront Charles.

                    JUDSON
          Yeah, what's up, man? I like that
          coat.

                    CHARLES ALEXANDER
          I do too.

                    JUDSON
          Take it off. I want it.

Cuzz punches Charles in the chin, and he staggers. Judson grabs Charles by the back of the coat and pulls out his Smith & Wesson 22 Caliber pistol.

                    JUDSON (CONT'D)
          This is a robbery. Don't make it a
          homicide.

Charles struggles to get loose from Judson, who puts the gun in his pocket. Cuzz punches Charles on the chin again, he goes down.

Robert Brooks Ballou Jr., who is a few yards ahead, turns and sees Charles on the ground. He starts running back toward Judson and Cuzz.

Judson sees Robert running towards him, he pulls the pistol out of his pocket, he prepares to shoot. To Judson's surprise, Robert runs right past him.

A few yards behind Judson, Cuzz, and Charles is Mac Thomas with a bunch of Compton Crip gang members. Robert runs right into them, they start beating him. Robert goes down, and the beating and stomping continue.

Standing thirty feet away, Bob Big Hawk Crear witnesses the shocking scene. It appears that Robert has been knocked out, he lies on the pavement mortally injured.

EXT. HOLLYWOOD - SUNSET BLVD - NIGHT

There are throngs of people on the scene when the police arrive. Uniformed Officers push the crowd back and tape off the area. Detective BOB SOUZA male Mexican 30s has arrived on the scene, he is approached by a UNIFORMED OFFICER.

                         BOB SOUZA
              What do we got?

                         UNIFORMED OFFICER
              Deceased black male, witnesses say
              he was robbed and beaten.

Bob Souza and the Uniformed Officer stand over the lifeless
body of Robert Brooks Ballou Jr.

EXT. LOS ANGELES POLICE STATION HOLLYWOOD DIVISION - NIGHT

Establishing shot of the BUILDING and MARQUEE.

INT. LOS ANGELES POLICE STATION HOLLYWOOD DIVISION - NIGHT

Seated at the desk of Detective AL GASTALDO male white 39. A
leery-looking 16-year-old male BLACK YOUTH #2 is being
questioned.

                         AL GASTALDO
              After you came out of the Concert.
              You saw the dead guy being beaten
              up?

                         BLACK YOUTH #2
                    (hesitant)
              I couldn't tell what was happenin'.

                         AL GASTALDO
              You were right there. Black guys
              right? How many were there?

                         BLACK YOUTH #2
              I don't know.

                         AL GASTALDO
              Do you know any of the black guys
              involved in the murder?

                         BLACK YOUTH #2
              Nah.

                         AL GASTALDO
                    (frustrated)
              I don't think you're being
              truthful.

Just then an angry heavy-set black woman in her 50s rumbles
in. This is GRANDMA, she confronts Al Gastaldo.

                    GRANDMA
          What's going on here?

                    AL GASTALDO
          Are you this kid's grandmother?

                    GRANDMA
          Yes, I am. Are you the officer
          that called me?

                    AL GASTALDO
          Yes ma'am. I'm detective Gastaldo.

                    GRANDMA
          What kind of trouble has my
          grandson gotten into?

                    AL GASTALDO
          Ma'am, your grandson witnessed a
          murder tonight. He's reluctant to
          answer my questions.

Grandma becomes incensed.

                    GRANDMA
          Boy, tell the man what you know.

Black Youth #2 shrugs his shoulders, then tilts his head
down.

                    GRANDMA (CONT'D)
          I ain't playing with you boy.
          Tell'em.

Black Youth #2 remains silent. Grandma moves in close, and
without warning, she slaps him hard.

                    GRANDMA (CONT'D)
          Tell him!

Then she slaps Black Youth #2 backhanded.

                    GRANDMA (CONT'D)
          Tell him!

Again she slaps Black Youth #2 forehanded.

                    GRANDMA (CONT'D)
          Tell him! Tell him what you saw!

Detective Al Gastaldo is stunned. Discombobulated Black
Youth #2 blurts out...

                         BLACK YOUTH #2
                The Crips! The Crips did it!

                         AL GASTALDO
                The Crips? What the hell are the
                Crips?

EXT. NEWSSTAND - MORNING

Amongst the various publications, front, and center, a
NEWSPAPER reads, Los Angeles Times, front-page headline:
Sunset-Vine Murder Gang Kicks Youth To Death in Street.

EXT. ST. ANDREWS PARK - DAY

A group of Crip Gang members is hanging out. Several Los
Angeles police squad cars pull into the parking lot. Bob Big
Hawk Crear is playing ping-pong when he is approached by
POLICE OFFICER #1.

                         POLICE OFFICER #1
                Can I see your ID?

Bob has a curious look on his face. He sits the ping-pong
paddle on the table reaches into his back pocket, pulls out
his wallet, then gives Police Officer #1 his ID. Police
Officer #1 looks at the ID, he hands it back to Bob.

                         POLICE OFFICER #1 (CONT'D)
                You, not the guy we're looking for.

Police Officer #1 questions several other youths in the park.
Bob walks over to the other side of the park where squad cars
are parked. He can clearly see James Cuzz Cunningham and
another youth in the back of the police squad car.

EXT. HOME OF JUDSON BACOT - MORNING

INSERT CARD: ONE WEEK LATER

Several police cars pull up. Officers rush up to the porch
and bang on the front door. The door opens, and MR. and MRS.
BACOT is stunned as Officers rush inside.

                         MR. BACOT
                Hey, what's goin' on?

OFFICER #4 hands Mr. And Mrs. Bacot some PAPERWORK.

                    OFFICER #4
          We have a warrant for the arrest of
          Judson Bacot.

Handcuffed, Judson Bacot is hustled out by two OFFICERS.
They shove Judson into the back of a squad car.

INT. HOME OF BOB CREAR - DAY

Bob Big Hawk has just walked in. Mrs. Crear is there to
greet him, she's holding a BUSINESS CARD in her hand.

                    MRS. CREAR
          The police were here earlier.

Mrs. Crear hands Bob the business card. The card clearly
shows the name, *LAPD Detective Al Gastaldo* on it. Bob gazes
at the business card. Looking bewildered he glances up at
Mrs. Crear.

INT. LOS ANGELES POLICE STATION HOLLYWOOD DIVISION - DAY

Bob Big Hawk walks in, he addresses a DESK OFFICER.

                    BOB BIG HAWK CREAR
          Excuse me, I'm trying to find
          Detective Al Gastaldo.

Bob hands the Desk Officer the business card. The Desk
Officer looks at the business card, he picks up the PHONE.

                    DESK OFFICER
          Al, there's a young man up front
          asking for you -- What's your name?

                    BOB BIG HAWK CREAR
          Bob, Bob Crear.

                    DESK OFFICER
          He says his name is Bob Crear --
          OK. Just a minute, he'll be right
          with you.

Seconds later, Al Gastaldo comes out with two UNIFORMED
OFFICERS.

                    AL GASTALDO
          Bob Crear?

                    BOB BIG HAWK CREAR
              (worried look)
          Yeah?

                    AL GASTALDO
          You're under arrest.

                    BOB BIG HAWK CREAR
          For what?

                    AL GASTALDO
          Murder.

                    BOB BIG HAWK CREAR
               (upset)
          That's bullshit man. You got the
          wrong dude.

The two Uniformed Officers restrain Bob.

                    BOB BIG HAWK CREAR (CONT'D)
          I'm telling you, man. I ain't
          murdered nobody.

Bob is handcuffed and led away.

EXT. RESIDENTIAL STREET - NIGHT

INSERT CARD: SUMMER 1972

The low tone of MUSIC can be heard coming from a HOUSE as Mac
Thomas sits on the hood of a car. Animated, Mac is talking
to Tam, Puddin, and several other Piru gang members. Tookie
walks over just when Mac Thomas launches into a tirade.

                    MAC THOMAS
          Cuz, this Piru Crip truce ain't
          gon' work.

                    TOOKIE
          Raymond ok'd that truce.

                    MAC THOMAS
          Either the Piru and Crip truce
          ends, or I'm gonna part ways with
          the Eastside Crips.

From the reaction of Tam and Puddin', they take exception to
Mac's attitude.

                    TOOKIE
          Calm down nigga.

MAC THOMAS
Raymond didn't talk to the Compton
Crips about ah truce. That puts me
and my homeboys at risk.

TOOKIE
I didn't know the Compton Crips
don't get along with the Pirus.

I/E. RESIDENTIAL STREET - HOUSE - NIGHT

MUSIC CUE: "Pop That Thang" by The Isley Brothers.

Buddha, Ricardo Bub Sims, and Herc are dancing with three
attractive ladies. The atmosphere is lively as the Crips and
Pirus party together. Suddenly, the party is interrupted by
the sound of breaking glass and shouting.

BUDDHA
This hat is mine now.

Buddha holding an ACE DUCE hat stands face to face with Lil
Vince.

LIL VINCE
Let's take it to the street!

Vince snatches the Ace Duce hat from Buddha's hand.

END MUSIC CUE:

SMASH CUT TO:

A chair crashes through the front window, and sounds of chaos
and breaking furniture are heard. People hurriedly scramble
outside, getting into cars and speeding away.

Buddha storms out the door, he's followed by Raymond
Washington, Ricardo Bub Sims, and Herc.

Mac Thomas leaps off the hood of the car. He and Tookie rush
over to Raymond.

TOOKIE
What happened?

RAYMOND
Buddha snatched Lil Vince's Ace
Duce off his head.

Lil Vince along with several Pirus rushes out the door with
GUNS drawn.

                    RAYMOND (CONT'D)
          Y'all be cool. Put the guns away.

                    LIL VINCE
          Fuck wrong with your homeboy
          startin' shit. Nigga tried to take
          my hat.

                    RAYMOND
          Buddha, you tryin' to break up the
          truce.

                    BUDDHA
          Bullshit! That's a lie!

                    MAC THOMAS
          Good. Ah, truce will never work.

                    RAYMOND
          I don't wanna hear that shit, Mac.
          I want this truce to work.

Mac Thomas gives Raymond Washington a hard stare. Mac pulls
Tookie to the side.

                    MAC THOMAS
          This truce with the Pirus, it's
          over.

EXT. NICKERSON GARDENS HOUSING PROJECT - APARTMENT - DAY

Standing in front is A.C. Bobalouie, Puddin', RHEA BOICE, an
18-year-old African American male, and TAVEE CLARK, also an
18-year-old African American male, are smoking weed and
drinking.

                    RHEA BOICE
          We ain't calling ourselves the
          green jackets no mo'.

                    TAVEE CLARK
          From now on call us the Bounty
          Hunters.

                    A.C.
          The Crips are growing fast. They
          outnumber other gangs. The Pirus
          want y'all to be down with us.

                    RHEA BOICE
          Fuck them crabs. The Bounty
          Hunters are down with the Pirus.

EXT. PUEBLO DEL RIO HOUSING PROJECT - DAY

Lorenzo is with GONROY, a male African American 18. Standing
around them are a bunch of tough looking hoodlums.

> LORENZO
> Gonroy, we need all off-brand gangs
> to unite against the Crips. The
> Piru Crip truce is fallen apart.

> GONROY
> The Bishops, we can't stand Crips.

> LORENZO
> The Bishops and the Pirus. We have
> to come together. It's the only
> way to fight the Crips.

> GONROY
> No problem. The Bishops and the
> Pirus are one.

I/E. LUEDERS PARK - GYMNASIUM - DAY

KIDS are playing basketball. Little GIRLS are roller
skating. Another group of kids is playing ping pong.

> SMASH CUT TO:

Just outside a gang meeting is taking place.

A.C. Bobalouie, Puddin', Tam, Vince, Gonroy, BIG COUNTRY,
male African American 19, ELGIN, male African American 19,
SLIM, male African American 18, MANIAC, male African American
18 and SMOKEY, male African American 18 indulge in a round of
drinking and drugs.

> BIG COUNTRY
> Them niggas killed Lil Country.

FLASHBACK:

EXT. HOUSE PARTY - 71ST STREET - NIGHT

Out front, LIL COUNTRY, a male African American 17, is firing
at CRIP GANG MEMBERS who return fire. Lil Country is shot in
the head, he drops dead. Several people rush to his side as
the Crip Gang Members run off into the darkness.

END OF FLASHBACK:

EXT. LUEDERS PARK - GYMNASIUM - NIGHT

A.C. Bobalouie, Puddin', Tam, Vince, Gonroy, Big Country,
Elgin, Slim, Maniac, and Smokey, are still drinking and
passing around marijuana joints.

                  A.C.
      Big Country, check this out. The
      Pirus is with you. Whatever the
      Brims wanna do. The Pirus is down.

                  LIL VINCE
      Slim, what's up with the Black P
      Stones?

                  SLIM
      That's why we here. The Black P
      Stones rollin' with the Brims and
      the Pirus.

                  TAM
      Maniac, Smokey. You feel the same
      way?

                  MANIAC
      We can hunt crabs right now.

                  SMOKEY
      I keep mah gat on me. I'm ready.

Smokey lifts his shirt up displaying a 38 REVOLVER tucked in
his waist.

                  ELGIN
      The Crips got to be sent a message.

I/E. SOUTH LOS ANGELES MORTUARY - DAY

A CASKET with the body of Brims gang member Lil Country is on
display. The family is seated on one side of the aisle.

Seated on the other side of the aisle are the Brims, Elgin,
Slim, Maniac, Smokey, and their homeboys. A viewing of the
body is taking place. The aisle is filled with mourners, one
by one they step up to pay their respects.

BLACK GUY #1 and BLACK GUY #2 in their late teens wearing
Khaki pants, waistline leather jackets, biscuit shoes, and
Ace Duce hats step up to view the body. Both Black Guys take
off their hats and bow their heads.

As they put back on their hats. Black Guy #1 takes his hand
and digs into the forehead of Lil Country, pulling out
mortician's wax from the bullet wound.

Black Guy #2 pulls out a small SPRAY PAINT CAN, he scrawls
the word Crip on the casket. Mourners are horrified, gasps,
and wails are heard, and some pass out. Elgin and the Brims
leap from their seats.

                    ELGIN
          Get them niggas!

Black Guy #1 and Black Guy #2 take off running. Elgin, Slim,
Maniac, Smokey, and their homeboys make chase.

                                        SMASH CUT TO:

The exit doors burst open. Black Guy #1 and Black Guy #2
come running out.

Almost immediately Elgin, Slim, Maniac, Smokey, and their
homeboys burst through the exit doors. Black Guy #1 and
Black Guy #2 turn to face the wrath of the Brims.

                    BLACK GUY #2
          Ca-rip!!!!!

Elgin, Slim, Maniac, Smokey, and the Brims swarm Black Guy #1
and Black Guy #2, giving them a savage beating.

INT. COMPTON POLICE DEPARTMENT - PRESS CONFERENCE - DAY

Camera crews and REPORTERS stand by. WHITE MAN #1 and WHITE
MAN #2 in their 50s, dressed in suits, stand next to a BLACK
MAN, 40s, wearing a shoulder holster and police badge.

                    WHITE MAN #1
          Gentlemen, in Compton, seventy
          thousand people live with a crime
          rate that is four times the
          national average. Municipal
          inaction, in the face of this
          monstrous crime wave, is a scandal.
          The federal government has poured
          seven million dollars in law
          enforcement assistance funds into
          Compton last year. But an on-the-
          spot investigation by the Compton
          Police Department indicates that
          the funds are either being wasted
          or misdirected. In a city that has
          seen thirty-one murders in the
          first six months of this year.
                    (MORE)

WHITE MAN #1 (CONT'D)
There were only five patrolmen and
one detective on the street during
last night's four-to-midnight
shift. Two of those patrolmen were
on traffic duty. Last night, we
observed twelve radio patrol cars
parked outside Compton police
headquarters. With no police
officers available to man them.
Such findings will be presented to
the Attorney General for the state
of California, Evelle J. Younger,
and to the United States Attorney
General Richard Kleindienst. The
state funnels federal laws and
federal funds for law enforcement
down to the local community. The
morale of the Compton Police
Department is absolutely zero.
Last night, the most experienced
patrolmen on the street had three
years on the job. Two of the men
riding alone in radio patrol cars
had less than a year's experience.
I am told that men with three days'
experience have been sent out on
homicide investigations.

REPORTER
Precisely, why did you come and
involve yourself in this matter?

WHITE MAN #1
Well as the newly elected president
of the international conference of
Police Association of which the men
of Compton belong. When they
acquainted us with their problem
here and the fact that the city
officials, were reluctant to step
in and try to rectify this
condition. We felt that the best
way that we could possibly give
them any kind of assistance at all
would be to come out here and bring
to light, this monstrous situation
is absolutely a cancer on society.

INT. APARTMENT - NIGHT

STEVE, a male African American 20, is shaking the dice. He
blows on them then throws the dice. The dice roll and hits
the wall, it's an eight.

                        STEVE
            Winner!

Steve picks up the money from the floor and counts it.

                        STEVE (CONT'D)
            I'm out of here.

MCCOY BROTHER #1 and MCCOY BROTHER #2, both male African
Americans in their 20s, aren't happy at all.

                        MCCOY BROTHER #1
            Man, I want a chance to win my
            money back.

                        MCCOY BROTHER #2
            You just can't leave like that. We
            want to gamble some mo'.

                        STEVE
            Gamble. I'm leaving.

Steve exits out the door.

EXT. APARTMENT - STREET - NIGHT

Steve, keys in his hand, walks up to his car. He attempts to
open the car door. Out of the darkness, McCoy Brother #1 and
McCoy Brother #2 approach with pistols drawn.

                        MCCOY BROTHER #1
            Hold it mutha fucka.

                        MCCOY BROTHER #2
            Give it up. The money, don't be
            stupid.

Steve reaches into his pocket, he pulls out a wad of money.
McCoy Brother #2 tucks his pistol away, then snatches the
money from Steve's hand.

                        MCCOY BROTHER #1
            Be cool man, turn around. Don't
            try nothin'.

McCoy Brother #1 and McCoy Brother #2 ease off into the
darkness, and FOOTSTEPS can be heard running away.

                        STEVE
                  (shouts)
            I'm gon' get you mutha fucka's.

EXT. LIQUOR STORE - 78TH AND CENTRAL AVENUE - NIGHT

Steve looking angry both hands in his coat pocket, lurks
around the front. He fiddles with a GUN that's tucked away
in his coat pocket.

INT. ORANGE 1967 CAMARO - NIGHT

Driving, Craig Craddock is with his girlfriend CLAIRETTE
female African American 17.

                    CRAIG
          Superfly was a cold movie.

                    CLAIRETTE
          Yeah, it was a pretty good movie.

                    CRAIG
          I'm gon' stop at the liquor store.

                    CLAIRETTE
          Don't tell me. You gon' get ah RC.

                    CRAIG
          RC Cola, got ah have it.

EXT. LIQUOR STORE - 78TH AND CENTRAL AVENUE - CONTINUOUS

The orange 1967 Camaro pulls next to the curb. Craig gets
out and notices Steve standing in front of the entrance.
Craig walks up to Steve and begins to harass him.

                    CRAIG
          Well, if it ain't Steve. What's up
          punk?

                    STEVE
          Don't fuck with me, Craig. You
          always fuckin' with me man. Stall
          me out.

Craig pokes Steve in the chest with his finger.

                    CRAIG
          Stall you out. You don't tell me
          what to do nigga.

                    STEVE
          Craig, I'm not in the mood. Stop
          fuckin' with me.

Craig spits on Steve. Steve pulls out his gun, he shoots
Craig in the chest twice. Steve runs over to the parking
lot, jumps in a TRUCK, he speeds off.

Clairette gets out of the Camaro, she rushes to Craig's side
as he lies on the pavement gurgling blood.

> CLAIRETTE
> My God. Hold on Craig, hold on
> Craig. Help! Somebody help!

I/E. 1968 CHEVY IMPALA - DAY

INSERT CARD: NOVEMBER 1972

A.C. Babalouie is driving down Rosecrans Avenue. He looks in
his rearview mirror and sees a Compton Police car tailing
him. The sound of the police siren chirps.

> A.C.
> Damn.

A.C. pulls over, the Compton Police car pulls just behind
him. Both doors of the Compton Police car swing open.
Officer Arthur Taylor, driver side, and Officer Shirley
Lidge, passenger side, are positioned behind the car doors.

Both Officers have their weapons drawn. Officer Taylor leans
into the police car and grabs the RADIO MICROPHONE. With one
hand on his weapon, and the other on the microphone.

> OFFICER TAYLOR
> Driver, exit the car with your
> hands up where we can see them.

A.C. gets out of his car with his hands held high.

> OFFICER TAYLOR (CONT'D)
> Driver, lay on the ground, face
> down, spread eagle.

A.C. goes down to his knees and lies prostrate on the ground.

> OFFICER TAYLOR (CONT'D)
> Lidge, go cuff him.

Officer Lidge, weapon pointed at A.C. approaches him
cautiously. She holsters her weapon, reaches for her
handcuffs, and places them on A.C. Officer Taylor holsters
his weapon, he hustles over to assist Officer Lidge. They
get A.C. to his feet.

                    A.C.
What's goin' on? Why y'all pull me
over? What'd I do?

Officer Taylor pats A.C. down, he pulls a WALLET from his
back pocket. Officer Lidge searches the car, and under the
front seat, she finds a PISTOL.

                OFFICER LIDGE
We got a weapon.

Officer Taylor shuffles through the wallet. He produces a
driver's license, and Taylor looks it over. Lidge emerges
from the car displaying the pistol.

                    A.C.
Y'all got to tell me something,
this is some bullshit!

Both Officers are silent as they place A.C. in the back seat
of the police car. Officer Taylor picks up the radio
microphone, as he holds A.C. Babalouie's driver's license.

                OFFICER TAYLOR
Dispatch, this is car four fifty-
two. We have one eighty-seven
suspect A.C. Moses in custody.

                DISPATCHER (V.O.)
Ten-four car four fifty-two.

A.C. handcuffed in the back seat is livid.

                    A.C.
What the fuck you talkin' bout one
eighty-seven! You got the wrong
mutha fucka, I'm telling you!

INT. TOOKIE'S MOTHER'S APARTMENT - LIVING ROOM - DAY

Seated on the couch. Tookie's mother Louisiana Williams is
on the telephone, she is speaking with Bob Simmons.

                BOB SIMMONS (V.O.)
Miss. Williams the court has
approved Stanley's enrollment into
the program.

                LOUISIANA WILLIAMS
Mr. Simmons, I can't thank you
enough, vouching for Stanley. The
judge gave him two choices. C.Y.A
or Youth Camp.

                         BOB SIMMONS (V.O.)
                    Factor Brookins is a camp for
                    wayward youths. We'll do our best
                    to help Stanley get his life back
                    on track.

I/E. HOME OF VIOLET SAMUEL - KITCHEN - EVENING

Derard is helping Violet put away groceries when there is a
KNOCK at the door.

                         VIOLET
                    I'll get that. Put the chicken in
                    the refrigerator. I'm gonna to
                    cook it tonight.

LAPD Officers Beno Hernandez and Robert Michael are standing
on the porch when Violet opens the front door. Violet is
taken aback to see the Officers standing there.

                         VIOLET (CONT'D)
                    What's goin' on officer?

                         ROBERT MICHAEL
                    Hello ma'am. I'm Officer Michael,
                    this is my partner Officer
                    Hernandez. We're trying to locate
                    Raymond Washington.

                         VIOLET
                    For what?

                         BENO HERNANDEZ
                    We have a warrant for his arrest.

Beno hands Violet the warrant, and she looks it over.

                         VIOLET
                    What's the arrest warrant for?

                         BENO HERNANDEZ
                    Robbery.

                         VIOLET
                    Raymond's not here.

                         ROBERT MICHAEL
                    Do you mind if we look around your
                    house?

Violet is hesitant.

                    VIOLET
        No. -- C'mon in.

Officers Beno Hernandez and Robert Michael walk in. Standing
in the LIVING ROOM, Derard sees them, he's surprised.

                    DERARD
        Mama, what're the cops doin' here?

                    VIOLET
        They lookin' for Raymond. I
        told'em they can look around.

Officers Beno Hernandez and Robert Michael begin their
search. They go from room to room. Derard and Violet sit
quietly on the Living Room couch. Hernandez and Michael
enter the Living Room.

                    ROBERT MICHAEL
        I guess we're through here ma'am.

The front door opens. Officers Beno Hernandez and Robert
Michael walk out and stand on the porch. Violet is standing
in the doorway.

                    BENO HERNANDEZ
        Sorry for the inconvenience.

                    ROBERT MICHAEL
        We'd appreciate it if you let us
        know when you see your son.

EXT. RESIDENTIAL STREET - HOUSE - EVENING

Two doors down from Violet Samuel's home. Staying out of
sight, Raymond Washington peers out from the side of a wall.
He can see Beno Hernandez and Robert Michael standing on the
porch talking to Violet.

EXT. WILSON PARK - COMPTON - DAY

A Yellow Bus is parked idling. A crowd of PARENTS and YOUTHS
are standing around when Tookie shows up with Louisiana
Williams.

Standing a few feet away smiling is Buddha, he is with his
mother MRS. MORROW female African American 40. Tookie greets
Buddha as their parents stand in the background chatting.

                    BUDDHA
        What's up Cuz?

                    TOOKIE
          The judge wanted to send me to
          C.Y.A. for a year. Some cat named
          Bob Simmons spoke up for me.

                    BUDDHA
          He's got the youth camp, Factor
          Brookins.

                    TOOKIE
          I guess it's better than C.Y.A.
          That's like a prison.

                    BUDDHA
          It's cool. We get furloughs.

                    TOOKIE
          What's that?

                    BUDDHA
          We get to leave the camp. Plus,
          some of the homeboys are there.
          Warlock, Monk, Melvin, other Crips.

The Youths begin boarding the Yellow Bus. Both Tookie and
Buddha hug their mothers.

                    LOUISIANA WILLIAMS
          Stanley, you stay out of trouble
          now.

                    TOOKIE
          Yeah, Mama.

                    MRS. MORROW
          Curtis, I don't want them people
          calling me about you. You hear me.

                    BUDDHA
          Alright, Mama, alright.

EXT. CALIFORNIA YOUTH AUTHORITY - DAY

Establishing shot of MARQUEE and facilities.

INT. CALIFORNIA YOUTH AUTHORITY - INMATE VISITING AREA - DAY

INMATES are socializing with their families. Seated at a
table A.C. Babalouie, MRS. MOSES female African American 45,
Tam, and Lil Vince. They are in good spirits.

                          A.C.
          Mama, I'm glad you brought them
          with you.

                          MRS. MOSES
          I wanted to surprise you.

                          TAM
          Babalouie! So what's up blood?

                          A.C.
          Blood?

Lil Vince makes a hand sign. His index finger and thumb make
a circle, the middle, ring, and pinky finger pointing
straight, as to form a "P".

                          LIL VINCE
          Yeah blood, how they treat'en you
          in here?

                          MRS. MOSES
              (suspicious)
          Y'all talkin' in code?

                          A.C.
          Street language Mama.

                          MRS. MOSES
          That's the shit that got you locked
          up. They couldn't tie you to a
          murder. But they got you on a gun
          charge.

A.C. Babalouie frowns, Lil Vince, and Tam look shamed.

EXT. HOME OF VIOLET SAMUEL - MORNING

Armed Police Officers have the place surrounded. Beno
Hernandez and Robert Michael use a MiniRam Breaching Tool.
The front door is forced open, and Officers rush in.

INT. HOME OF VIOLET SAMUEL - BEDROOM - MOMENTS LATER

Lying in her bed asleep, Violet is awakened by the commotion.
Suddenly the BEDROOM DOOR violently burst open. Police
Officers rush in and wrest Violet from the bed.

Raymond Washington half-dressed is subdued as police enter
his room. Derard can only watch as he cringes in a corner.

EXT. HOME OF VIOLET SAMUEL - MOMENTS LATER

Beno Hernandez and Robert Michael march a half-dress Raymond
Washington to an awaiting squad car.

Violet and Denard come out of the front door. Standing on
the porch looking helpless, they watch as the police put
Raymond into the squad car.

INT. COURTROOM - DAY

INSERT CARD: TWO WEEKS LATER

The JUDGE is seated behind the bench. Raymond Washington is
seated at the defendant's table. Seated next to Raymond
PUBLIC DEFENDER #1. Sitting in the gallery, Violet and
Denard have a look of uncertainty.

                    JUDGE
          Mr. Washington, you waived your
          right to a jury trial? I have
          reviewed all the evidence in your
          case. I'm going to adjudicate you
          guilty of aggravated robbery.

Raymond shoots up from his chair.

                    RAYMOND WASHINGTON
               (exclaims)
          This is some bullshit. I ain't
          robbed nobody.

The Judge strikes his gavel.

                    JUDGE
          Counsel control your client.

The Public Defender #1 stands up and cautiously grabs Raymond
by his shoulder.

                    PUBLIC DEFENDER #1
          Raymond calm down. Please, sit
          down.

Scowl on his face, Raymond eases back down into his seat.

                    PUBLIC DEFENDER #1 (CONT'D)
          Your honor, I would just ask that
          the minimum sentence that the court
          allows be considered.

The Public Defender #1 sits back down.

                    JUDGE
          Mr. Washington, I'm sentencing you
          to six years maximum, with a
          minimum sentence of three years in
          state prison.

Raymond is visibly upset, again he shoots up from his seat
and lashes out.

                    RAYMOND
          I've been railroaded.   I've been
          railroaded got damn it.

The BAILIFFS quickly restrain Raymond, they usher him out.

Violet can only look as tears stream down her face. A
dejected Derard tries to comfort her.

INT. MARTIN LUTHER KING HOSPITAL - EMERGENCY ROOM - DAY

INSERT CARD: APRIL 6TH, 1973

PARAMEDICS rush two black male GUNSHOT VICTIMS in on gurneys.
Two UNIFORMED OFFICERS are accompanying the paramedics.

INT. LOS ANGELES POLICE SOUTHEAST STATION - DAY

Police OFFICERS have three male juvenile African-Americans in
handcuffs. This is GANG SUSPECT #1, GANG SUSPECT #2, and
GANG SUSPECT #3. The Police Officers are approached by
DETECTIVE #5 and DETECTIVE #6.

                    DETECTIVE #5
          Take them to separate interrogation
          rooms.

INT. INTERROGATION ROOM #1 - DAY

Seated at a small table. GANG SUSPECT #1 has a mean attitude
prominently displayed on his face. Detective #5 and
Detective #6 walk in, they sit directly across from Gang
Suspect #1.

                    DETECTIVE #6
          Witnesses identified you as being
          on the campus of Locke High School.

                    GANG SUSPECT #1
          So.

                    DETECTIVE #5
          You're a Crip gang member, right?

                    GANG SUSPECT #1
          Nah.

Detective #6 gets up from his seat. He walks around the
small table and gets right in the face of Gang Suspect #1.

                    DETECTIVE #6
          You're going to confess to the
          murders.

                    GANG SUSPECT #1
          I ain't confessin' to shit.

That response prompts an unrestrained ass-whipping from
Detective #6.

INT. INTERROGATION ROOM #2 - DAY

We see the same situation. Detective #5 and Detective #6
walk in, they mean business. The two Detectives don't bother
sitting down. GANG SUSPECT #2 is sitting at a small table
looking unnerved.

                    DETECTIVE #5
          So what happened?

                    GANG SUSPECT #2
          I don't know what you talkin' bout.

                    DETECTIVE #6
          You and your two Crip buddies
          walked onto the Locke High School
          Campus and murdered two students.

                    GANG SUSPECT #2
               (smug)
          Like I said. I don't know what you
          talkin' bout.

The two Detectives, looking pissed off, turn to each other.

                    DETECTIVE #6
          Should I do it, or do you wanna do
          it?

                    DETECTIVE #5
          No, I'll do it.

Detective #5 reaches across the small table. He aggressively
grabs Gang Suspect #2 and pulls him out of the chair dragging
him across the table. Detective #5 then commences to dish
out a vicious beating to Gang Suspect #2.

INT. INTERROGATION ROOM #3 - DAY

Again, Detective #5 and Detective #6 walk in. Detective #5,
shirt collar opened, tie loosened. He takes a handkerchief
and wipes his slightly bruised knuckles.

Gang Suspect #3, looking tuff, but puzzled. Detective #6
just smiles at Gang Suspect #3, as Detective #5 tucks the
handkerchief in his breast coat pocket.

                    DETECTIVE #5
               (snide)
          Ok, which of you Crips killed the
          two students?

Gang Suspect #3 sits in silence. Detective #6 slams both
hands down onto the small table. He leans forward giving
Gang Suspect #3 a hard stare.

                    DETECTIVE #6
          Witnesses have identified all three
          of you as shooters. So what
          happened?

                    GANG SUSPECT #3
          I ain't got nothin' to say.

                    DETECTIVE #6
          You sure about that?

                    GANG SUSPECT #3
          Yeah.

Detective #6 grabs Gang Suspect #3 by his collar, stands him
up, and delivers a powerful blow to the face. Gang Suspect
#3 falls back up against the wall, he slides down to the
floor.

Detective #6 walks around the table, picks Gang Suspect #3 up
off the floor, and again Detective #6 delivers a punch to the
face.

This sends Gang Suspect #3 flying over the table, he lands at
the feet of Detective #5 who begins kicking Gang Suspect #3
in the gut.

                    DETECTIVE #5
          Talk you black bastard, talk.

Detective #5 continues with the gut kicks.

> GANG SUSPECT #3
> Ok, Ok, Ok!

> DETECTIVE #5
> Ok, what?

> GANG SUSPECT #3
> I'll talk.

FLASHBACK:

EXT. LOCKE HIGH SCHOOL - ATHLETIC FIELD BLEACHERS - DAY

GEORGE EASTER, 17, male African-American, and ELLIS HUGHEY, 18, male African-American are hanging out smoking weed.

> GEORGE EASTER
> (hitting the joint)
> Ellis, this some good shit man.

> ELLIS HUGHEY
> Yeah, it is. Now pass the joint
> George, you hoggin' the weed nigga.

George passes the joint to Ellis, he takes a long drag, inhales, holds it, then blows out the smoke.

> ELLIS HUGHEY (CONT'D)
> Yeah, that's what I'm talkin' bout.

Out of nowhere Gang Suspect #1, Gang Suspect #2, and Gang Suspect #3 come walking up brandishing REVOLVERS.

> GANG SUSPECT #1
> What's up cuz?

> GANG SUSPECT #2
> What set you from nigga?

Ellis is so shaken, he drops the joint. Wide-eyed, both Ellis and George are completely speechless.

> GANG SUSPECT #3
> Fuck the Athens Park Boys.

Gang Suspect #1, Gang Suspect #2, and Gang Suspect #3 begin shooting. Ellis and George turn away to run but are gunned down.

END OF FLASHBACK:

INT. INTERROGATION ROOM #3 - DAY

Lying on the floor, Gang Suspect #3 is in a fetal position.
Detective #5 and Detective #6 stand over him.

                    GANG SUSPECT #3
              That's it, that's what happened.

INT. PARKER CENTER DOWNTOWN LOS ANGELES - DAY

INSERT CARD: NOVEMBER 30TH, 1973

Chief EDWARD M DAVIS, a white male 57, and Assistant Chief
DARRYL GATES, a white male 47, stands before a board of
commissioners.

                    EDWARD M. DAVIS
              Los Angeles is in the grip of a
              gang crisis, and the situation will
              probably get worse. Gangs are
              terrorizing citizens and police
              manpower which should be used to
              combat other crimes is being
              drained to combat young hoodlums'
              activities.

Chief Davis steps to the side of the podium. Assistant Chief
Gates steps to the microphone.

                    DARRYL GATES
              Thank you, Chief Davis. Most of
              you know me, I'm Assistant Chief
              Darryl Gates. I'd like to direct
              your attention to these pictures
              and the map we have.

Gruesome images of victims are shown. A map of the city
highlighting areas of gang concentration is seen.

                    DARRYL GATES (CONT'D)
              The increase in black gangs is due
              to the demise of such groups as the
              Black Panthers and the US
              Organization. These militant
              groups and other black
              organizations gave the youths some
              place to focus their energy. South
              Los Angeles is sectioned off.
                         (MORE)

DARRYL GATES (CONT'D)
You have the East Side, watts,
Compton, the Westside, and
Inglewood. According to our
investigators, there are probably
twenty-seven different chapters of
the Crips, the most notorious black
gang. Other gangs have sprung up
to protect themselves from the
Crips. Approximately twelve major
gangs formed in the South Central
area for self-survival against the
Crips. Some of these rival gangs
refer to themselves as bloods. The
body of commissioners has received
reports of all types of fear
existing in some parts of the city,
in schools, and neighborhoods.
Today's briefing at Parker Center
is a beginning. We can make
informed judgments as to what the
department should be doing to deal
with gangs.

EXT. CALIFORNIA YOUTH AUTHORITY - DINING AREA - DAY

A.C. Babalouie, food tray in hand, is in the chow line. Rhea
Boice walks up holding a food tray.

RHEA BOICE
What up homeboy?

A.C.
(surprised)
Rhea, blood, what you doin' up in
here?

RHEA BOICE
Probation violation.

Looking around, some Crips do not appreciate the reunion.
One angry CRIP INMATE steps to A.C. Babalouie and Rhea.

CRIP INMATE
Aye, cuz, y'all save that shit for
later.

Rhea gives the Crip Inmate a hard look. A.C. Babalouie
defensive posture is ready for action.

A.C.
Nigga, we can get down right now.

A.C. Babalouie, big for his age, gives an intimidating look.
The Crip Inmate looks at A.C. Babalouie and backs off.

                    CRIP INMATE
          I'll deal with you later nigga.

EXT. CALIFORNIA YOUTH AUTHORITY - YARD - DAY

A.C. Babalouie is in the midst of a meeting. Amongst him is
six CYA inmates.

Rhea Boice, MICHAEL FORD, male African American 17, KENNY
TRASH, male African American 16, ARTHUR PURDLE, male African
American 17, ANGELO, male African American 16, and JENNINGS,
male African American 17.

                    A.C.
          Crips outnumber the non-Crip gangs
          in here.

                    RHEA BOICE
          Crips outnumber non-Crip gangs
          period. In here and on the
          streets.

                    MICHAEL FORD
          So what we spose to do?

                    KENNY TRASH
          Dudes in here that don't bang are
          forced to join the Crips.

                    A.C.
          The Brims, Pirus, Bounty Hunters,
          Bishops. All non-Crips, we have to
          unite. If we don't, we got no
          chance.

                    ARTHUR PURDLE
          Babalouie -- we'll still be
          outnumbered.

                    A.C.
          Start using the word blood.

                    ANGELO
          Blood?

                    A.C.
          Yeah, that's how we identify each
          other. If ah nigga say Cuz, you
          know he ah Crip. We use blood, you
          know the dude ain't ah Crip.

                    JENNINGS
          So blood, for non-Crip gangs, is
          like saying cuz?

                    A.C.
          Exactly, so, spread the word blood.

INT. APARTMENT BUILDING - TOOKIE'S ROOM - DAY

Tookie stands in front of the mirror. He looks over his
attire: Godfather hat, ducktail button-down dress shirt,
black waistline leather coat, heavily starched Levi's with a
small cuff, and Stacy Adams biscuit shoes. Tookie's mother,
Louisiana Williams, walks in.

                    LOUISIANA WILLIAMS
          Where you goin'?

                    TOOKIE
          Out.

                    LOUISIANA WILLIAMS
          Bob Simmons let you out on
          furlough. Don't get in any
          trouble.

As if he can't hear his mother. Tookie continues to admire
himself in the mirror.

                    LOUISIANA WILLIAMS (CONT'D)
          I don't want you to end up like
          Curtis.

                    TOOKIE
          You mean Buddha.

                    LOUISIANA WILLIAMS
          Yeah -- well, he left the camp on
          furlough, got in trouble, now he's
          dead. I don't want that to happen
          to you.

Tookie turns from the mirror and looks at his mother.

                    TOOKIE
          Don't worry, It won't.

I/E. LIQUOR STORE - SOUTH LOS ANGELES - DAY

Four CRIP GANG MEMBERS are standing at the counter. From the
glass display case, the CASHIERS grab several GOLF HATS.
Small metal clubs are prominent on the front of the hat.

He grabs BLUE HANDKERCHIEFS with a distinctive pattern. The
Cashier places the items on the counter. The Crip Gang
Members grab the Golf Hats, Handkerchiefs, they proudly put
on the Golf Hats.

They neatly fold the Blue Handkerchiefs and tuck them in the
left-back pocket of their Levi's so they hang down.

The four Crip Gang Members walk out the door like soldiers.
With a distinct gangsta limp, they stroll down the street.

EXT. ST. ANDREWS PARK - DAY

A throng of Crip gang members has amassed themselves. Like
an emperor, Tookie walks through the crowd as they part like
the Red Sea. Tookie steps on top of the picnic table looking
down on the mass of Crip gang members.

                    TOOKIE
          The Crips have become ah
          unstoppable force. They talkin'
          bout the Crips on the news, in the
          paper. Like the military, cats is
          join'in the Crip's every day. You
          know what ain't cool. Different
          Crip sets is poppin' up all ova'
          L.A. Ain't checkin' with Raymond,
          nobody Checkin' with me. Niggas
          just think they can start a set,
          and call they'selves Crips. That
          shit ain't happen'en, not long as
          I'm around. Raymond started the
          Crips, now he in the pen. Mac
          Thomas ran the Compton Crips, he
          locked up doing time. It's up to
          me to lead -- me, Tookie -- I'm the
          leader of the Crips. Eastside,
          Westside, Compton -- we all one
          gang -- Crips.

The mass of Crip gang members pledges solidarity with a
resounding roar, YEAH! A few gang members in the crowd shout
the name TOOKIE, and a few more gang members shout TOOKIE.

Now the whole mass of Crip gang members is shouting, TOOKIE!
TOOKIE! TOOKIE! Standing atop the picnic table, Tookie
basks in the adoration of his Crip subjects.

EXT. DEUEL VOCATIONAL INSTITUTION STATE PRISON - DAY

INSERT CARD: FEBRUARY 1974

On the SOFTBALL FIELD, a game is underway. Raymond
Washington is at bat. The PITCHER tosses the ball, and
Raymond swings hitting a grounder. He races down the first
baseline.

The SHORTSTOP scoops up the ground ball, he throws it to
first base. Raymond is out! As Raymond turns to trot back
to the dugout. Before he can, BLACK MILITANT #1 gets
Raymond's attention.

> BLACK MILITANT #1
> Hey, you.

Raymond turns back towards the unrecognized voice. Standing
alongside Black Militant #1 is BLACK MILITANT #2, and BLACK
MILITANT #3.

> BLACK MILITANT #1 (CONT'D)
> We need to talk.

The three Black Militants walk right up to Raymond.

> RAYMOND
> What.

> BLACK MILITANT #1
> We belong to the BGF, the Black
> Guerilla Family.

> RAYMOND
> So.

> BLACK MILITANT #1
> I don't like what you doin' in
> here.

> RAYMOND
> Cuz, I don't care what you like.

> BLACK MILITANT #2
> That shit you started on the
> streets. The Crips, it stops right
> here.

> BLACK MILITANT #3
> Stop recruiting Crips in here.

A group of BLACK INMATES is watching the game. They notice
the tension between Raymond and the three Black Militants.
The group of Black Inmates, with purpose, walk over to
Raymond.

They stand right behind Raymond giving the three Black
Militants angry looks, leading to a Mexican standoff.

INT. TORRANCE SUPERIOR COURT - DAY

Appearing from an adjacent door. Judge BURCH DONAHUE, a
white male 40s walks in, the BAILIFF steps forward.

>   BAILIFF
>   All rise. Judge Burch Donahue
>   presiding.

Everyone in the gallery, defendant JESSE R. HENRY 17, male
African American, PUBLIC DEFENDER #2, and the prosecuting
ATTORNEY, all stand. Judge Donahue takes a seat behind the
bench. Everyone in unison sits down.

>   JUDGE DONAHUE
>   "Jesse Henry and his legal counsel,
>   please stand."

Both Jesse Henry and Public Defender #2 stand.

>   JUDGE DONAHUE (CONT'D)
>   Jesse Henry you were found guilty
>   of two counts each of first-degree
>   murder and first-degree robbery.
>   Before I hand down sentencing. I
>   have a few things to add. Mr.
>   Henry, you are 17, the crimes that
>   you and two other minors committed
>   are heinous, to say the least.
>   This justified you being tried as
>   an adult in a non-jury trial. You
>   murdered a housewife for three
>   dollars, killed a young father for
>   ten dollars...

MONTAGE:

EXT. HOUSE - NIGHT

INSERT CARD: 8 PM MAY 7TH 3703 W. 102ND ST., INGLEWOOD
CALIFORNIA

LUCILLE PRICE 36, a female African-American has just pulled
into her driveway. Henry and two MALE YOUTHS African-
Americans, ages 15 and 14 drag Lucille from her car.

They beat her severely and take her purse then Henry shoots
Lucille in the face. The three young assailants take her CAR
and flee the scene.

While driving they look through Lucille's purse only to
discover it contains three dollars.

EXT. 16TH AND ALAMEDA - NIGHT

INSERT CARD: LESS THAN AN HOUR LATER

A big rig truck pulls to the curb. WILLIE C MILNER male
white 30s gets out. He walks up to a payphone.

Henry, holding a pistol, emerges from the shadows with two
Male Youths. They confront Rob Milner and rob him of $225.
Henry threatens Milner's life but does not shoot.

EXT. DOWNTOWN GARMENT DISTRICT - NIGHT

JUAN AGUILAR 29, a male Mexican is leaving an upholstery
shop. Henry and the two Male Youths attack Aguilar robbing
him of $10. Aguilar is subsequently shot in the head by
Henry.

EXT. GOLDEN STATE FREEWAY ON RAMP - NIGHT

INSERT CARD: LATER THAT EVENING, 10 PM

An abandoned car is blocking southbound Glendale Boulevard.
A Highway Patrol OFFICER runs the license plate.

EXT. SURFACE STREETS - NIGHT

INSERT CARD: ONE HOUR LATER 11 PM

An LAPD SQUAD CAR is cruising the area. OFFICERS spot Henry
and the two Male Youths walking. The squad car quickly pulls
up, Officers jump out, guns drawn. The youths, still armed,
put up no resistance and are arrested.

END MONTAGE:

INT. TORRANCE SUPERIOR COURT - DAY

Judge Donahue, is still behind the bench.

                    JUDGE DONAHUE
          Mr. Henry, you have a lengthy
          record. You were arrested at 14
          for petty theft, arrested for being
          in the presence of marijuana,
          curfew violation, battery,
          loitering on school grounds,
          attempted burglary, five counts of
          attempted murder, possession of a
          concealable firearm, carrying a
          firearm, and, finally, murder.
          Police investigators say you are
          deeply involved with a youth gang
          called the Crips. Prior to the May
          7th murder spree with the other two
          youths, 14 and 15. Mr. Henry, you
          had gone through a series of
          counseling sessions with juvenile
          authorities. You were placed on
          probation once and repeatedly
          released back into the custody of
          your parents. I'm at a loss for
          words. Maybe the system failed
          you, or your parents, society could
          be partly to blame -- Mr. Henry, I
          hereby sentence you to life. Your
          sentence is to be carried out in
          the California Department of
          Corrections prison system.

Judge Donahue strikes his gavel. WEEPING can be heard as the
Bailiff escorts Jesse R. Henry through an adjacent side door.

INT. DEUEL VOCATIONAL INSTITUTION STATE PRISON - CELL - DAY

Raymond Washington is lying on his bunk when Black Militant
#1, BLACK MILITANT #2, and BLACK MILITANT #3 show up. Black
Militant #1 holds a NEWSPAPER, he tosses it at Raymond.

                    BLACK MILITANT #1
          What do you have to say for
          yourself?

Raymond picks up the Newspaper. The front page reads, *Youth,
17, Gets Life Sentence for Killing 2 Persons for $13.*
Raymond ponders for a moment.

                    BLACK MILITANT #2
          Two black kids, fourteen and
          fifteen also participated in the
          murders.

                    BLACK MILITANT #3
          Guess what gang they claim? --
          Crip.

                    BLACK MILITANT #1
          You're responsible for fuck'en up a
          lot of young black lives.

Raymond tosses the Newspaper back at the three Black
Militants. The three Black Militants rush Raymond, they
fight furiously.

Raymond puts Black Militant #1 on his back. Black Militant
#2 throws a punch, Raymond blocks it, and he counters with a
right punch. This sends Black Militant #2 reeling backward
out the door.

Black Militant #3 pulls out a SHANK, he lunges at Raymond.
Fending off attempted stabs, Raymond grapples with Black
Militant #3 who continually thrust the shank.

PRISON GUARDS rush in to break up the fight, they subdue
Black Militant #3. Winded, panting, Raymond is bleeding,
he's been stabbed in the shoulder.

INT. DORMITORY ROOM - NIGHT

INSERT CARD: DECEMBER 10TH, 1974 EASTLAKE JUVENILE HALL

As inmates lie asleep in their bunks. In the dark, a 17-year-
old African American male, JUVENILE #1 is prying a METAL
FIXTURE from a wall.

Juvenile #1 breaks the Metal Fixture from the wall, he then
takes it and smashes a one-foot square window. A BLACK TEEN
INMATE is awakened.

                    BLACK TEEN INMATE
          Hey, what are you doin'?

                    JUVENILE #1
          Be quiet, go back to sleep.

Juvenile #1 tosses a blanket through the window and then
proceeds to squeeze through the one-foot square opening.

EXT. DORMITORY ROOM - CONTINUOUS

Juvenile #1 is now in the outdoor fenced area, he is staring at a 20-foot fence. Juvenile #1, blanket in his arm, begins to scale the fence.

At the top of the fence, he tosses the blanket on top of the barbed wire. Juvenile #1 climbs over the blanket onto the other side of the fence, he scales down to the ground. Juvenile #1 escapes into the night, he's gone.

EXT. MANUAL ARTS HIGH SCHOOL - 42ND STREET - DAY

A CAR pulls up to the curb.

INT. CAR - DAY

Behind the wheel is DENNIS CHEATHAM male African American 18. With him is Juvenile #1 and another teen, this is a 16-year-old African American male, JUVENILE #2. Cheatham hands each juvenile a PISTOL.

                    DENNIS CHEATHAM
          Knock them fools off.

EXT. MANUAL ARTS HIGH SCHOOL - CAMPUS - DAY

It's lunchtime, STUDENTS are walking about. Juvenile #1 and Juvenile #2 walking at a deliberate pace, head to the lunch area. Once there they confront ANTHONY MACK 16, African American male and, CHARLES RILEY 17, African American male.

                    JUVENILE #1
          Hey nigga, what set you from?

                    ANTHONY MACK
          What you talkin' bout cuz?

                    CHARLES RILEY
          You trippin' nigga.

Juvenile #1 and Juvenile #2 draw their guns on Mack and Riley.

                    JUVENILE #1
          This Family, blood. Fuck Crip.

Juvenile #1 fires his pistol shooting Mack, killing him instantly. He then shoots Riley in the stomach. The two Juveniles take off running.

EXT. MANUAL ARTS HIGH SCHOOL - 42ND STREET - CONTINUOUS

Cheatham is sitting in the getaway car. Juvenile #1 and
Juvenile #2 come running up, and they jump in the car.
Cheatham pulls off, the tires burning rubber.

EXT. LOS ANGELES COUNTY BOARD OF SUPERVISORS - DAY

Establishing shot of the building.

INT. LOS ANGELES COUNTY BOARD OF SUPERVISORS - OFFICE - DAY

KENNETH HAHN, a white male 54, is seated behind his desk.
Sitting across from Hahn is chief probation officer CLARENCE
CABELL, white male 40s. Cabell hands Hahn a MANILA FOLDER,
upon opening...

                    CLARENCE CABELL
          That's a complete case history of
          the juveniles who were involved in
          the senseless murder at Manual Arts
          High School.

                    KENNETH HAHN
          All three of the youths arrested
          had long police records. The 17-
          year-old triggerman has a record of
          23 prior arrests. The 16-year-old
          youth arrested has twelve prior
          arrests, including six felonies.
          The 18-year-old arrested, Dennis
          Cheatham. Had twenty-two prior
          arrests according to police.

Cabell cringes and has an ambivalent look on his face.

                    KENNETH HAHN (CONT'D)
          Clarence, you're Chief of the
          Probation Department. This killing
          shouldn't have happened. A judge
          of the juvenile court or a
          probation officer should have
          spotted a serious pattern earlier.

Frustrated, Hahn tosses the Manila Folder on his desk.

                    CLARENCE CABELL
          Mr. Hahn, this is a systemic
          problem. Case overload, the
          juvenile courts are completely
          backed up.

EXT. SENATE OFFICE BUILDING - DAY

INSERT CARD: APRIL 23RD, 1975 WASHINGTON D.C.

A press conference is taking place. At the Podium stands
BIRCH BAYH, a male white 57. Behind him stands a group of
POLITICIANS made up of Men and Women. Birch Bayh holds up a
thick MANUAL.

>   BIRCH BAYH
>   Today the Senate sub-committee is
>   releasing a preliminary report on
>   violence and vandalism in our
>   public schools. The evidence
>   compiled by the sub-committee drawn
>   from seven hundred and fifty school
>   districts around the country is
>   enough to turn one's stomach. The
>   Congressional body has concluded
>   that violence and vandalism has
>   reached a level of crisis.
>   Violence and vandalism in our
>   schools cost five hundred million a
>   year. Equal to all the money spent
>   on school books in 1972. Schools
>   across our nation are experiencing
>   serious crimes of a felonious
>   nature, including brutal assaults
>   on our teachers and students, as
>   well as rapes, extortion,
>   burglaries, and thefts. An
>   unprecedented wave of wanton
>   destruction and vandalism.

Reporters begin to clamor. DONALD P. MYERS, white male 38,
steps forward hand raised. Birch Bayh points at him.

>   DONALD P. MYERS
>   Donald Myers United Press
>   International. Senator Bayh, what
>   specific solutions are suggested in
>   the report?

>   BIRCH BAYH
>   The nation's school districts are
>   spending millions of dollars
>   annually to fight school crime.
>   This is just a preliminary report
>   further hearings will be conducted.

Another reporter steps through the clamor, hand raised. This
is JAMES J. KILPATRICK, male white 55. Birch Bayh nods his
head acknowledging Kilpatrick.

                    JAMES J. KILPATRICK
          James Kilpatrick Universal Press
          Syndicate. You mentioned violence
          and vandalism has reached a level
          of crisis. It's not unreasonable
          to ask that preliminary remedies be
          recommended.

                    BIRCH BAYH
          Many solutions have been offered.
          More discipline by both parents and
          teachers, better education methods,
          more police security, and
          personnel.

                    JAMES J. KILPATRICK
          Senator Bayh, the gangs. How will
          you deal with gangs in the schools?

                    BIRCH BAYH
          The schools of Los Angeles report
          one "gun incident" every other day.
          In 1971, 72, warfare among the
          city's estimated one 150 gangs saw
          29 students dead. One of the
          largest Los Angeles gangs is called
          the Crips. The name is a short
          form of Cripples which derived from
          the gang's trademark of maiming or
          crippling their victims. The Crips
          also have two auxiliary units. The
          Criplettes, composed of girl
          members, and the Baby Crips, made
          up of elementary and Jr. High
          school children. The sub-committee
          will recommend ten billion in
          federal anti-vandalism grants be
          spent on more cops and additional
          school security.

EXT. CALIFORNIA YOUTH AUTHORITY - DROM - DAY

INSERT CARD: OCTOBER 10TH, 1975

Hurriedly, A.C. Babalouie exits the door. He practically
bumps into ALVIN TRESVANT, a male African American 18.

                    ALVIN TRESVANT
          Babalouie, I need to talk to you.

A.C. Babalouie, turns, walking at an angle.

                    A.C.
          Alvin, I'm in a rush. I got
          visitors waiting for me in the
          visitor's room.

                    ALVIN TRESVANT
               (serious look)
          It's about Tam.

A.C. Babalouie hurried pace comes to a halt.

                    A.C.
          What about Tam?

Alvin Tresvant walks up to A.C. Babalouie.

                    ALVIN TRESVANT
          He was killed last night.

A.C. Babalouie grabs Alvin Tresvant by his shirt collar.

                    A.C.
          What the fuck are you talkin' bout?

Alvin Tresvant slowly removes A.C. Babalouie's hands from his
shirt collar.

                    ALVIN TRESVANT
          Tam was standing in front of his
          house...

FLASHBACK:

EXT. PIRU STREET - TAM'S HOUSE - NIGHT

Tam is hanging out with two FRIENDS, they appear to be
talking. Two BLACK TEENS on BICYCLES, casually peddling,
ride up the street.

Tam, along with his two friends, is engaged in banter and is
oblivious to the Black Teens on Bikes. The Two Black Teens
stop directly across from Tam and his Friends.

They pull out PISTOLS from their waistbands and begin
shooting. Before Tam can react he is shot, the two Friends
flee as bullets narrowly miss them.

The two Black Teens tuck the pistols away and speedily ride
off. Tam, dead, eyes open, lies on the pavement with a
bullet in his forehead.

END OF FLASHBACK:

EXT. CALIFORNIA YOUTH AUTHORITY - DROM - DAY

A.C. Babalouie is in a stupefied state.

> ALVIN TRESVANT
> (echoing voice)
> Babalouie, you alright man?

A.C. Babalouie shakes himself out of the stupor.

> A.C.
> I can't believe this shit. You
> hear anything else? Who did it?

> ALVIN TRESVANT
> Nah, man. That was it.

INT. DEUEL VOCATIONAL INSTITUTION STATE PRISON - DAY

INSERT CARD: JANUARY 1976

PHONE to his ear, Raymond Washington sits in a BOOTH looking
through the GLASS PARTITION. On the other side of the Booth,
Phone to his ear, sits ROSEY GREER, male African American 44.

> ROSEY GRIER
> You'll be getting out in a few
> months. What's the plan?

> RAYMOND
> Your guess is as good as mine.

> ROSEY GRIER
> What kind of answer is that?
> Without a plan, you could end up
> back in here, or worst, dead.

> RAYMOND
> Mr. Greer, why are you taking all
> this interest in me?

> ROSEY GRIER
> Raymond, I played eleven seasons in
> the NFL, for two different teams.
> The Los Angeles Rams and the New
> York Giants. Since I retired, I've
> dedicated my life to serving
> others.
> (MORE)

                    ROSEY GRIER (CONT'D)
          I founded "American Neighborhood
          Enterprises," a nonprofit
          organization that serves inner-city
          youth like yourself. I'm a
          minister, I'm here to minister to
          you.

                    RAYMOND
          You sound like my mother. Always
          preaching.

                    ROSEY GRIER
          Maybe you shoulda listened to her.

                    RAYMOND
          Yeah, you're probably right.

                    ROSEY GRIER
          The change starts right now. But
          it's up to you to make that change.

                    RAYMOND
          I definitely don't wanna end up
          back in here.

                    ROSEY GRIER
          I can help you get a job when you
          get out. You have any kids?

                    RAYMOND
          I have a son.

FLASHBACK:

INT. HOSPITAL - ROOM

Raymond looking amazed stands next to the bed. Pee Wee, a
smile on her face, lies in the bed holding a newborn BABY
BOY.

Raymond carefully takes the Baby Boy from Pee Wee's arms.
This strong young man, proudly, ever so gently, rocks the
baby in his arms.

END OF FLASHBACK:

INT. DEUEL VOCATIONAL INSTITUTION STATE PRISON - DAY

The phone still to his ear, Raymond has a melancholy look.
Rosey, the phone still to his ear, appears optimistic.

                    ROSEY GREER
          Cheer up. You have a lot to be
          thankful for. Learn from the past,
          look forward to the future.

INT. THE PALM HOUSE - LIVING ROOM - EVENING

A hand pops a CASSETTE into a BOOM BOX, the finger pushes
play.

MUSIC CUE: "Who'd She Coo?" by Ohio Players

An attractive young black woman, this is CLEO 22, and a few
Criplettes are hanging out.

Also hanging out, wearing hot pants, revealing tops, and go-
go boots are some LADIES of leisure.

Kicking back and sitting on the couch is Tookie, sitting next
to him is GODFATHER, a male African American 23. Cleo joins
them, she sits next to Tookie.

END MUSIC CUE:

                    GODFATHER
          I'm tellin' you man pimpin' is easy
          money.

The sexy lips of a Lady of leisure wrap around a cigarette.

                    TOOKIE
          Godfather, cuz, I'm not interested.
          I stay high too much to focus on
          pimpin'. Crippin' means more to me
          than pimpin'.

Cleo slides in close to Tookie.

                    CLEO
          Why you think we got these ladies
          here?

                    TOOKIE
          Cleo, when I got out of camp in
          seventy-three, Bob Simmons gave me
          a job here, as a counselor. I
          don't have to worry bout a place to
          stay, buying food, or paying bills.
               (to Godfather)
          The Palm House is the perfect place
          for me. I'm in Compton, I get paid
          to lift weights and counsel Crips.

                    GODFATHER
          I hear you cuz.

Criplette SALLY walks up, a pretty 22-year-old African
American female.

                    SALLY
          Tookie, I need to talk to you cuz.

                    TOOKIE
          What's up?

                    SALLY
          Privately, cuz.

Tookie walks over to a corner with Sally.

                    TOOKIE
          What?

                    SALLY
          You need to watch yo back. The
          Pirus out to get you.

                    TOOKIE
          How you know?

                    SALLY
          I hear things. I was kickin' it at
          this dude's crib, he's a Piru.
          Them niggas like me. They be
          tryin' to talk to me.

                    TOOKIE
          So you fuckin' with Pirus? You
          wanna be a Piru?

                    SALLY
          Hell Nah, it's Crip or Die.

                    TOOKIE
          I ain't worried bout them niggas.

INT. HOME OF VIOLET SAMUEL - DAY

The front door opens. In walks Violet, followed by Raymond.
They are greeted by Reggie, Derard, Donald Ray, and Ronald
Joe.

                    REGGIE
          Raymond!

Raymond is all smiles as he hugs each one of his brothers, a smile shines from Violet's face too.

                    DERARD
          I'm glad you're back home, bro.

                    RAYMOND
          Damn, man. You done got tall, what
          are you, 18 now?

                    DERARD
          Yep.

Ronald Joe looks fit in his military uniform.

                    RAYMOND
          You made it through Vietnam.

                    RONALD
          Thank God -- You made it through
          prison.

                    RAYMOND
             (sigh)
          Yeah -- I guess I should be
          thankin' God too.

                    VIOLET
          You better thank God. He kept you
          alive this long.

                    RAYMOND
          I hear you, mama, I hear you.
          Reggie, Donald Ray. What's up with
          y'all?

                    REGGIE
          Just Working, been at the same job
          since you went in, driving a
          forklift.

                    RAYMOND
          I can dig it. So Donald, you
          working man?

                    DONALD
          Yeah, I got a decent factory job.
          It pays the rent.

                    RAYMOND
          Cool, that's real cool man.

                         VIOLET
          Son -- what are your plans, now
          that you're out?

                         RAYMOND
          You sound like somebody I know.
          Matter fact, I got a Job interview,
          RCA records.

The family is elated.

                         VIOLET
          How'd you manage that?

                         RAYMOND
          Rosey Grier set it up.

                         DERARD
          The football player?

                         RAYMOND
          Ex-football player. He has a non-
          profit foundation that helps inner-
          city youth.

                         VIOLET
          Praise the Lord! Praise the Lord!

EXT. RCA RECORDS - SUNSET BLVD - MORNING

Establishing shot of the BUILDING as cars traverse the
street. Raymond Washington walks into the entrance.

INT. RCA RECORDS - RECEPTION AREA - DAY

A RECEPTIONIST sits behind a desk thumbing through job
applications when Raymond walks up.

                         RAYMOND
          Excuse me, I have an appointment
          with Mr. Hershel Gill.

The receptionist stops what she's doing.

                         RECEPTIONIST
          Just one minute.

The Receptionist picks up the receiver and then pushes a
button on the multi-line office phone.

INT. RCA RECORDS - OFFICE - DAY

GLASSES on, sitting behind a desk studying job applications
is HERSCHEL GILL, a white male 40. The BUZZER on his multi-
line office phone goes off, and he picks up the receiver.

> HERSCHEL GILL
> Yes -- OK, send him in.

Within seconds the door opens. A slightly nervous Raymond
Washington enters. Herschel Gill takes off his Glasses.

> RAYMOND
> Hello Mr. Gill, I'm Raymond
> Washington.

> HERSCHEL GILL
> Hello Raymond, I've been expecting
> you. Have a seat.

Raymond takes a seat directly across from Herschel Gill.

> HERSCHEL GILL (CONT'D)
> Raymond, I'm the head of Human
> Resources here at RCA. I was
> contacted by Rosey Grier. He
> filled me in on your situation,
> being recently released from
> prison.

> RAYMOND
> Mr. Grier visited me often.

> HERSCHEL GILL
> Yes -- RCA has committed to hiring
> selected individuals referred by
> Mr. Grier's non-profit program.
> Helping former inmates -- reducing
> recidivism.

> RAYMOND
> I appreciate the opportunity.

> HERSCHEL GILL
> That's great. I personally want to
> help minorities excel in life. I'm
> going to give you an entry-level
> position.

> RAYMOND
> Ok, what's next?

> HERSCHEL GILL
> Can you start today?

                    RAYMOND
          Today?

                    HERSCHEL GILL
          Yes, today.

                    RAYMOND
          Oh, yeah, I'm ready.

                    HERSCHEL GILL
          Good. You'll need to fill out a
          job application. You will be
          working in the mailroom.

Herschel Gill picks up the receiver, he pushes the button on
the multi-line office phone.

                    HERSCHEL GILL (CONT'D)
          Have Mr. Washington fill out an
          application. Then send him to the
          mailroom, thank you.

Herschel Gill hangs up the receiver.

                    HERSCHEL GILL (CONT'D)
          OK, Raymond. See the receptionist,
          she'll get you situated.

                    RAYMOND
          Thank you, Mr. Gill. I won't let
          you down.

                    HERSCHEL GILL
          I'm sure you won't.

Both Raymond and Herschel Gill stand up from their seats, and
they shake hands. Raymond walks out the door, Herschel Gill
sits back down, places his glasses on, and glances at some
paperwork.

INT. THE PALM HOUSE - BEDROOM - NIGHT

Tookie is lying in bed with Sally watching TV.

                    TOOKIE
          I'm gon' take the dog for a walk.
          I'll be back in a little while.

                    SALLY
          OK, I'll be here.

INT. THE PALM HOUSE - LIVING ROOM - NIGHT

Tookie walks in. Godfather, MADBULL, male African American
21, and TERRIBLE TEE, male African American 21, are hanging
out.

>   TOOKIE
>   Aye, man, y'all can take off.

>   MADBULL
>   You sure cuz?

>   TOOKIE
>   Madbull, cuz, I'm cool.

>   TERRIBLE TEE
>   You want some privacy with Sally,
>   huh?

>   GODFATHER
>   We should stay. The Palm House got
>   a reputation. It's the boy's home
>   where the Crips hang out.

Tookie pulls out a 38 SPECIAL from behind his back.

>   TOOKIE
>   This'll keep me safe.

Tookie reaches into his pocket, he pulls out some Car Keys.
He tosses them to Godfather.

>   TOOKIE (CONT'D)
>   Take my Chevy. Terrible Tee,
>   Madbull, roll out with Godfather.
>   I'll catch y'all later.

Godfather, Madbull, and Terrible Tee all look at each other
with uncertainty.

>   GODFATHER
>   Alright, cuz, later.

EXT. THE PALM HOUSE - BACKYARD - NIGHT

Wearing a LEATHER MAXI COAT, Tookie puts a leash on his PIT
BULL. He walks the dog out of the back gate.

EXT. RESIDENTIAL STREET - COMPTON - NIGHT

Tookie, walking with his Pit Bull, smokes a marijuana joint.
In the distance, HEADLIGHTS can be seen from a car.

Tookie continues walking with the pit Bull as the car slowly pulls alongside him. A group of DARK FIGURES can be seen checking Tookie out. Tookie realizes something is up, he puts his hand in his coat pocket, and the car pulls off.

EXT. THE PALM HOUSE - FRONT YARD - NIGHT

Tookie takes a seat on the porch, lying beside him is a PUMP SHOTGUN. There is an unnatural peacefulness in the air, as the Pit Bull runs around. Tookie takes a drag from a marijuana joint.

Tookie stands up and grabs the pump shotgun, hearing the Pit Bull growling and barking. He looks towards the sound, but it's too dark to see anything, so he turns to check in the opposite direction.

The darkness lights up with gunfire. Tookie dives to the ground and crawls to the side of the house, he pulls the 38 Special from his coat pocket. Tookie struggles to his feet, he takes aim, but the shooters have vanished.

Grimacing, Tookie's legs wobble as he falls back to the ground. In the faint light, semi-conscious, Tookie feels his legs and notices blood all over both hands.

Tookie tries to look at his hands; they are out of focus, and he falls unconscious. Sally cautiously comes out of the front door and stands on the porch in total shock.

INT. HOSPITAL - PATIENT ROOM - DAY

Tookie wakes up to a smiling Sally peering down at him and rubbing his head.

                    SALLY
          He's alive, folks.

Standing next to Sally is Raymond Washington.

                    RAYMOND
          Yeah, I see, but what I want to
          know is what we gon' do about this.

                    TOOKIE
          Raymond?

                    RAYMOND
          In the flesh.

                    TOOKIE
          When did you get out the pen?

                    RAYMOND
          A couple of weeks ago.

                    TOOKIE
          How'd you find out I got shot.

                    RAYMOND
          Word travels. Who did it?

                    TOOKIE
          I don't know.

Godfather gets up from a chair.

                    GODFATHER
          I think it was the Pirus. They hip
          to The Palm House.

                    RAYMOND
          Whoever did it, they gon' pay.

Tookie looks down at his torso, both legs are in casts.

                    TOOKIE
          Can't pay back nobody with my legs
          like this.

                    SALLY
          You gon' be fine baby. Give it
          some time, you'll be good as new.

                    GODFATHER
          Yeah Tookie cuz, soon as you back
          on yo feet cuz. We gon' get the
          niggas who shot you.

In pain, Tookie frowns at Godfather.

                    TOOKIE
          The way my legs feel, I'm not sure
          if I'll be able to walk again.

                    RAYMOND
          I'm pissed cuz, all these different
          Crip sets done popped up while I
          was in prison. Ah, different
          leader for each new set. Niggas
          giving the Crips a bad name.

                    TOOKIE
          I hear you cuz. What we started is
          out of control.

INT. RCA RECORDS - OFFICE FLOOR - DAY

Raymond is pushing a mail cart. He places mail on the desks
of various EMPLOYEES.

INT. RCA RECORDS BUILDING SUNSET BLVD - MAILROOM - AFTERNOON

Raymond comes in with the mail cart. MISS BARNES, a white
female 32, approaches Raymond with a stack of FORMS.

                    MISS BARNES
          In the morning I need you to take
          these memos to the heads of each
          department, business affairs,
          legal, art, A&R, publicity,
          marketing, sales, and label
          liaison.

Miss Barnes hands Raymond the forms.

                    RAYMOND
          OK, no problem.

                    MISS BARNES
          I'm clocking out. I'll see you
          tomorrow.

                    RAYMOND
          See you tomorrow Miss Barnes.

I/E. 61 CHEVY IMPALA LOWRIDER - EVENING

MUSIC CUE: "Get Da Funk Out Ma' Face" by The Brothers Johnson

Raymond cruises down the street in his 61 Impala. A police
car gets behind Raymond, he's being tailed. Raymond looks in
his REARVIEW MIRROR...

                    RAYMOND
          Damn.

The police squad car's lights flash. Raymond slows down and
pulls over to the side of the road.

END MUSIC CUE:

Both police officers get out of the squad car. POLICE
OFFICER #2 cautiously approaches Raymond's driver's side
window. POLICE OFFICER #3 maintains the rear.

>   RAYMOND (CONT'D)
>   What's the problem officer?

>   POLICE OFFICER #2
>   May I see your driver's license,
>   please?

>   RAYMOND
>   What did I do?

>   POLICE OFFICER #2
>   Your driver's license sir.

Frustration shows on Raymond's face, he reaches into his back
pocket. Police Officer #2 watches Raymond closely, his hand
on his revolver.

Raymond pulls out his wallet, he produces the driver's
license. Raymond hands it to Police Officer #2, who examines
it and then hands it back to Raymond.

>   POLICE OFFICER #2 (CONT'D)
>   Would you step out of the car,
>   please?

>   RAYMOND
>   (upset)
>   For what?

Police Officer #2, hand on his revolver.

>   POLICE OFFICER #2
>   Step out of the car Mr. Washington,
>   sir.

Raymond reluctantly gets out of the car.

>   POLICE OFFICER #2 (CONT'D)
>   Turn around and put your hands
>   behind your back.

>   RAYMOND
>   Man, this is some bullshit.

Police Officer #3 hand on his revolver, walks over to join
his partner.

                    POLICE OFFICER #2
          I'm not going to ask you again.
          Turn around, put your hands behind
          your back.

Raymond complies, he turns around, hands behind his back.
Police Officer #2 places handcuffs on Raymond.

                    RAYMOND
          What the fuck is goin' on man.

                    POLICE OFFICER #2
          You're under arrest.

                    RAYMOND
          For what?

                    POLICE OFFICER #2
          Suspicion of burglary.

INT. OFFICE OF CITY COUNCILMAN - DAY

INSERT CARD: JANUARY 1977

ROBERT FARRELL, male African American 40, angered, stands
behind his desk. Confronting Farrell are LAPD Officers, and
GREGORY FOWLER, male white 32.

                    ROBERT FARRELL
          Mr. Fowler, or whatever your name
          is. You can't just barge in here
          making demands.

                    GREGORY FOWLER
          Councilman Farrell, I've been
          tasked by the District Attorney's
          Office to audit the books of
          Project Long Table and its parent
          company Project Heavy.

ERNEST SPRINKLES, a male African American 25, walks in on the
heated exchange.

                    ERNEST SPRINKLES
               (concerned)
          Hey, what's goin' on here?

Attention turns to Ernest.

                    ROBERT FARRELL
          They want to audit my books -- This
          is Ernest Sprinkles. He's
          treasurer of Project Heavy.

                    GREGORY FOWLER
          Just the man I need to see.

                    ERNEST SPRINKLES
          Do you have a search warrant?

                    GREGORY FOWLER
          I'm investigating Project Long
          Table, the anti-gang violence
          program launched last April with a
          grant of $91,581 dollars provided
          through the Mayor's Office of
          Criminal Justice Planning.

Gregory Fowler sifts through file cabinets and pores over
documents, LAPD Officers take photographs of financial
records. Robert Farrell and Ernest Sprinkles can only watch.

                    GREGORY FOWLER (CONT'D)
          There have been allegations of
          embezzlement and misuse of funds.

                    ROBERT FARRELL
          Which are completely unfounded.

                    GREGORY FOWLER
          This investigation stems from an
          October eighteenth shooting
          incident during which project
          coordinator Bennie Ray Simpson led
          an alleged shotgun attack on rival
          gang members.

FLASHBACK:

INT. PROJECT LONG TABLE OFFICE - 46TH AND BROADWAY - DAY

TERRENCE SCOOBY LEE, male African American 22, along with
several BRIMS GANG MEMBERS walk in. Bennie Ray Bulldog
Simpson, male African American 22, sits behind a desk.

He is surrounded by Deadeye Clint Willis, HENRY J. WILDS,
male African American 22, and CARLOS RAULS, male African
American 19.

                    TERRENCE SCOOBY LEE
          I'm looking for Bennie Ray Simpson.

                    BULLDOG
          Who are you?

                    TERRENCE SCOOBY LEE
          Scooby -- me and my homeboys, we
          Brims.

Bennie Ray Bulldog Simpson gives off a nonchalant look.
Clint, Henry, and Carlos look unfazed.

                    TERRENCE SCOOBY LEE (CONT'D)
          You ever heard of me?

                    BULLDOG
          Nah. But I know about the Brims.

                    TERRENCE SCOOBY LEE
          I heard you the coordinator of
          Project Long Table.

Bennie Ray Bulldog Simpson with a calm silent pause.

                    TERRENCE SCOOBY LEE (CONT'D)
          I also heard you ah Crip.

                    BULLDOG
          Is that right?

                    TERRENCE SCOOBY LEE
          I need you to approve funds to pay
          for the funeral of a Brims gang
          member. Jimmy Celestin, he was
          nineteen. Jimmy was shot and
          killed two days ago.

                    CLINT WILLIS
          Cuz, I heard somethin' about that.

Terrence Scooby Lee glares at Clint.

                    TERRENCE SCOOBY LEE
          Who is you, blood.

                    CLINT WILLIS
          Deadeye Clint, the resource
          coordinator. -- Sorry, I don't
          think we can help.

                    TERRENCE SCOOBY LEE
          Blood, this program is backed by
          the city to reduce violent conflict
          between street gangs. Y'all got
          the money.

                    HENRY J. WILDS
          Clint, is that in our budget?
          Payin' for funerals?

                    CARLOS RAULS
          Bulldog, you have to check with
          Councilman Farrell.

                    BULLDOG
          You right, I do.

                    TERRENCE SCOOBY LEE
          You niggas are full of shit.
          Project Long Table is a front. You
          mutha fucka's ain't tryin' to help
          nobody but yourselves. Stickin'
          money in yo own pockets.

                    BULLDOG
          Our funds don't cover funerals,
          cuz.

                    TERRENCE SCOOBY LEE
               (defiant)
          Yeah, well we ain't leavin' till we
          get some money to bury our dead
          homeboy.

                    BULLDOG
          You ain't gettin' shit.

Terrence races around the desk, he swings on Bennie Ray
Bulldog Simpson. A full-blown fight breaks out, Henry
tussles with Terrence. Clint grabs a bat swinging it at two
Brims Gang Members.

Carlos comes out of nowhere brandishing a SHOTGUN. Terrence
and the Brims Gang Members scramble out the front door.

EXT. PROJECT LONG TABLE - 46TH AND BROADWAY - CONTINUOUS

Terrence frantically runs out the front door, the Brims Gang
Members are right behind him. Carlos runs out the front door
wielding the Shotgun. He takes aim... BOOM!

END OF FLASHBACK:

INT. OFFICE OF CITY COUNCILMAN - DAY

LAPD Officers put away the camera and place folders back in file cabinets. Looking perplexed, Ernest Sprinkles turns to Robert Farrell.

Robert Farrell gasps and drops down in his seat. Rubbing his forehead, Farrell looks up at Gregory Fowler.

> GREGORY FOWLER
> The misuse of funds and
> embezzlement allegations came to
> light during interviews with
> witnesses, victims, and suspects
> involved in the shooting incident.

EXT. RURAL COMMUNITY IN TEXAS - MORNING

Sparsely populated and pleasant in nature, homes are spread out from one another, while cattle and horses graze on the grass. One particular house becomes the focus.

INT. GRANDMOTHER HOUSE - KITCHEN - MORNING

Raymond Washington's GRANDMOTHER, a female African American 70, is frying bacon. Violet walks in, she takes over.

> VIOLET
> Mama let me do that. You sit down
> and relax.

Grandmother a bit agitated, waives off Violet.

> GRANDMOTHER
> Violet move out the way. I been
> doin' this before you was born.

> VIOLET
> No mama, that's why me and Raymond
> came to Texas. To look after you,
> now have a seat.

Grandmother slowly moves to the table and sits down.

> GRANDMOTHER
> I'm not indolent. I can still do
> things for myself.

Violet gets some eggs from the refrigerator.

> VIOLET
> Yes, you can.

Violet gets a bowl from the cabinet and cracks some eggs.

                    VIOLET (CONT'D)
          But ain't no spring chicken.

INT. GRANDMA'S HOUSE - LIVING ROOM - MORNING

Sitting on the couch. Raymond is on the PHONE talking with a
HOMEBOY.

                    RAYMOND
          I needed to get away from L.A. The
          police was fucken' with me all the
          time. Arrested me on a bunk
          burglary charge, held me for
          seventy-two hours. I lost my job
          behind that shit. Talkin' bout
          mistaken' identity.

                    HOMEBOY (V.O.)
          We need you back in L.A. The Crips
          is out of control, no leadership.

                    RAYMOND
          Man, them cats ain't gon' listen to
          me.

                    HOMEBOY (V.O.)
          You started this shit, cuz. If
          anybody can pull the Crips
          together, you can.

                    RAYMOND
          Mom's wanted me to come to Texas
          with her, to help my Grandmother.

                    HOMEBOY (V.O.)
          You hip to Project Long Table?

                    RAYMOND
          That's Bulldog, involved with some
          anti-gang program.

                    HOMEBOY (V.O.)
          He's in the paper, some shootin'
          with the Brims at his office.

                    RAYMOND
          That's what I'm talkin' bout, no
          unity. The Crips gon' always get
          blamed.

A voice BLARES from the kitchen, it's Violet.

> VIOLET (O.S.)
> Raymond! Breakfast is ready.

Raymond pauses.

> RAYMOND
> Gotta go, I'll catch you later.

INT. HOSPITAL - EXAMINATION ROOM - DAY

A CAST SAW cuts through the plaster cast on Tookie's leg.
Tookie reclines on the examination table as DOCTOR #1
carefully removes the cast.

> DOCTOR #1
> How do your legs feel?

Tookie bends his legs. He wiggles his ankles and toes.

> TOOKIE
> They feel pretty good.

> DOCTOR #1
> Try to stand up.

Tookie sits on the edge of the examination table. Looking
apprehensive, with help from Doctor #1. Tookie eases off the
examination table onto his feet.

> DOCTOR #1 (CONT'D)
> You OK?

> TOOKIE
> Yeah -- My legs are a little weak.

> DOCTOR #1
> That's to be expected. I decided
> to leave the bullets in your feet.
> Removing them would have caused
> more damage.

> TOOKIE
> Wow.

> DOCTOR #1
> You were lucky not to have lost a
> foot. You'll walk with a permanent
> limp though.

> TOOKIE
> I don't believe that Doc.

>   DOCTOR #1
> Well, that's what you're facing.

>   TOOKIE
> Doctors have been wrong before.

EXT. PROJECT HEAVY BUILDING - DAY

INSERT CARD: LOS ANGELES SEPTEMBER 1977

Raymond Washington, dressed for an interview, walks in from off the street.

INT. PROJECT HEAVY - OFFICE - DAY

Raymond attentively listens as he sits in front of JOHNNY R. ODOM, a male African American in his mid-30s, who is seated behind a desk.

>   JOHNNY R. ODOM
> Project Heavy is a city-run
> government program. I'm the
> assistant director for anti-
> vandalism.

>   RAYMOND
> I heard about Project Heavy. They
> had some problems working with
> Project Long Table. It was in the
> newspaper, a shooting went down
> that involved Bennie Simpson.

>   JOHNNY R. ODOM
> Yeah, well, ah. Bennie Simpson was
> in charge of Project Long Table, an
> affiliate of Project Heavy. Bennie
> was recently acquitted on all
> charges.

>   RAYMOND
> Uh, OK.

>   JOHNNY R. ODOM
> Look, Raymond, we want to employ
> young people like yourself.

>   RAYMOND
> Like myself -- cats that run with
> gangs -- ex-cons.

                    JOHNNY R. ODOM
          If you want to put it that way,
          yeah. The job entails cleaning up
          alleys, buildings that have been
          defaced with graffiti. It pays
          minimum wage.

                    RAYMOND
          I need the money. I just moved
          back to L.A. from Texas.

                    JOHNNY R. ODOM
          So you'll take the job?

                    RAYMOND
          Hell yeah, I'll take the job.

Johnny reaches across the desk extending his hand, Raymond
responds by shaking it.

INT. SLATER HOUSE BOYS HOME - LIVING ROOM - DAY

Surrounded by the usual suspects, Godfather, Mad Bull, and
Terrible Tee, Tookie is bench-pressing 250 lbs.

Also on hand are several Criplettes, Bad Bessie, Pretty
Connie, Cookie, Cleo, and Big Pam. Mad bull standing behind
the bench press, hands and arms extended, spots Tookie.

                    MAD BULL
          Seventeen, eighteen, c'mon two
          more, nineteen, twenty.

Tookie lets the barbell rest on the bench press rack, he
stands up flexing his bulging muscles.

                    TERRIBLE TEE
          You look like Mr. Olympia.

                    BAD BESSIE
          Tookie you should enter a contest.

Tookie struts around, flexing as if in a body-building
contest.

                    TOOKIE
          Arnold Schwarzenegger told me the
          same thang at Venice Beach -- And
          just think, that Doctor said I'd
          have a permanent limp.

Just then BOB SIMMONS, a male African American 35, walks in
the front door. Tookie takes a break from showcasing his
muscles.

>   TOOKIE (CONT'D)
>   Bob, what's up?

>   BOB SIMMONS
>   Hey brotha, I need to talk to you.

>   TOOKIE
>   Is every thang cool?

>   BOB SIMMONS
>   Yeah, just wanna rap for a minute.

Bob sits with Tookie at the Dining Table.

>   BOB SIMMONS (CONT'D)
>   I want you to meet someone.

>   TOOKIE
>   Who?

>   BOB SIMMONS
>   A guy that runs a youth program.
>   It's for individuals involved in
>   gangs to promote peace.

>   TOOKIE
>   (frowns)
>   C'mon Bob, we been down this road.
>   I'm cool on youth programs.

>   BOB SIMMONS
>   I run a youth program. A boys
>   home, you're involved with that.

>   TOOKIE
>   That's different, I trust you.
>   Them other cats just tryin' to make
>   money. I don't wanna deal with
>   dudes from other gangs either.

Bad Bessie stands a few feet away listening.

>   BOB SIMMONS
>   (frustrated)
>   I don't understand you, man. I've
>   kept you out of jail. Made you a
>   counselor at three of my Boys
>   Homes. The Red House, Slater
>   House, The Palm House, put you on
>   salary -- What you do.
>   (MORE)

                         BOB SIMMONS (CONT'D)
                    Recruit Crips right out my boys
                    home. Get the Red House shut down,
                    that's money out of my pocket.
                    Cats tried to kill you at The Palm
                    House. I'm funded by the
                    government, you realize that.

                         TOOKIE
                    Yeah, man.

                         BOB SIMMONS
                    It's hot in Compton. The heat
                    ain't just on you, it's on me too.

Bad Bessie walks up.

                         BAD BESSIE
                    Excuse me Mr. Simmons, but I been
                    listening. I have a suggestion.

                         TOOKIE
                    Bessie, stay out of this.

                         BAD BESSIE
                    Tookie, it ain't gon' hurt to
                    listen to whoever it is he wants
                    you to meet.

                         BOB SIMMONS
                    Just hear this guy out Tookie,
                    that's all I'm asking.

Tookie, elbow on the table, chin in his hand, just stares.

EXT. ALLEY SOUTH CENTRAL L.A. - MORNING

A PICKUP TRUCK pulls up, on its door we see a COUNTY OF LOS
ANGELES logo. The door swings open, and out steps PETE, a
male black, 40.

                         PETE
                    Let's get to it.

Stepping out of the Pickup Truck, wearing work clothing, is
Raymond Washington, JOSE, male Latino 20, RENE, female black
19, LANCE, male black 19.

                         PETE (CONT'D)
                    Raymond, get the paint buckets.
                    Rene, Lance, you two work with
                    Raymond. Grab the paintbrushes and
                    rollers.
                              (MORE)

>   PETE (CONT'D)
>   Paint over graffiti on all the
>   walls. Jose, you workin' with me,
>   grab trash bags and rakes.

Raymond, Rene, and Lance get the paint buckets, brushes, and
rollers from the Pickup Truck. Jose grabs the trash bags and
rakes.

>   JOSE
>   Aye, Pete, Mexican for lunch?

>   PETE
>   Sure, everybody, Mexican food for
>   lunch.

>   LANCE
>   Jose, you don't like soul food?

>   JOSE
>   We had that yesterday.

>   PETE
>   Raymond, take Rene and Lance, start
>   at that end. Jose we'll start
>   picking up trash at the other end.

Raymond carries the paint bucket while Rene and Lance handle
the paintbrushes and rollers.

One particular wall stands out with gang graffiti. *N-Hood* is
scrawled on a wall and crossed out on the same wall with blue
spray paint is the word *Family*.

>   LANCE
>   Damn, blood, that shit ain't cool.

>   RENE
>   Blood? What you mean cuz?

Scrawled in red spray paint is the word *Family*, crossed out
on the wall is the word *N-Hood Crab*.

>   RENE (CONT'D)
>   Niggas done crossed out da set.

>   LANCE
>   Oh, that's a problem, crossen' out
>   Inglewood Family. Crab ass niggas.

>   RENE
>   Fuck you, slob! This N-Hood!

Raymond has to get between Rene and Lance.

                    RAYMOND
          Alright, be cool. What y'all know
          about gang bangin'?

                    LANCE
          Enough to blast a crab.

                    RENE
          Niggas in red come up dead.

                    RAYMOND
          Y'all got shit fucked up. Lance,
          do you know how Inglewood Family
          got started?

                    LANCE
          Nah, and I don't care. I'm from
          Inglewood, and I'm down with
          Family.

                    RAYMOND
          The Gladiators, Inglewood Family
          used to be called the Gladiators.
          Rene, what you know about N-Hood?

                    RENE
          What you mean?

                    RAYMOND
          Where they come from? Who started
          N-Hood?

                    RENE
          What is this? A lesson on gangs?

                    RAYMOND
          You two would kill each other. For
          what? For colors? Red, Blue?

Lance and Rene both suck their teeth.

                    RAYMOND (CONT'D)
          Lance, who started the bloods?

                    LANCE
          Ah man, c'mon with that bullshit.

                    RAYMOND
          Rene, who started the Crips?

                    RENE
          Fuck if I know. You tell me.

                         RAYMOND
          I did when I was fifteen years old.
          Y'all heard of Tookie?

                         LANCE
          Yeah, he got a rep. I heard of'em.

                         RENE
          Everybody knows Tookie.

                         RAYMOND
          I hooked up with Tookie in seventy-
          one. He ran the west side Crips, I
          ran the east side Crips. Compton
          Crips came from the east side
          Crips. All the black gangs that
          wasn't Crips united to fight
          against the Crips. The Pirus,
          Brims, Bounty Hunters, Bishops,
          Family. The Crips outnumbered them
          all.

Lance and Rene pay a little closer attention.

                         RAYMOND (CONT'D)
          Crips started to use the word cuz,
          that's how they recognize each
          other. Black gangs that wasn't
          Crips, started saying blood, that's
          how they identified each other.
          Same thing with the handkerchiefs,
          Crip wore blue rags in the left-
          back pocket. Bloods started
          wearing red rags.

Lance begins to clap.

                         RAYMOND (CONT'D)
          Thanks for the speech.

At the other end of the alley, Pete looks up from raking up
trash. Jose, gloves on, stops picking up trash, and he looks
up.

                         PETE
          What the hell are they doing?

                         JOSE
          Looks like they talkin'.

                         PETE
          I can see that.
              (yells)
          Hey, get to work down there.

Raymond turns, and he acknowledges Pete with a wave.

                    RAYMOND
          C'mon, let's get to work. Dunk
          them rollers, paint over that
          graffiti.

Rene and Lance start painting over the graffiti-laden wall.

                    RENE
          I'm ah paint over the red.

                    LANCE
          I'm gon' paint over the blue.

                    RAYMOND
          Just paint, damn it, paint.

EXT. AVALON GARDENS HOUSING PROJECT - PARKING LOT - DAY

A 1968 Chevy Impala pulls in. A collection of cookie-cutter
neatly manicured homes is seen. Tookie and Godfather get out
of the car. They walk down a pathway up to the front door of
one particular home.

Tookie KNOCKS on the door.

INT. AVALON GARDENS HOUSING PROJECT - BAD BESSIE'S HOME - DAY

Bad Bessie opens the door, standing there is Tookie and
Godfather.

                  BAD BESSIE
       Come on in.

Tookie and Godfather walk in. Standing behind Bad Bessie is
the burly 6 foot 5 inch Rosey Grier, a gentle smile dawns on
his face.

                  ROSEY GRIER
       Which one of you guys is Tookie?

                  TOOKIE
       Me.

Rosey extends his hand, Tookie shakes it.

                  ROSEY GRIER
       Rosey Grier, what's happening
       brotha?

Rosey extends his hand to Godfather, and they shake.

              ROSEY GRIER (CONT'D)
What's yo name brotha?

              GODFATHER
Godfather.

Bad Bessie looks, and rubs her brow.

              ROSEY GRIER
Godfather?

              GODFATHER
Yeah.

              ROSEY GRIER
OK.

Rosey turns to Bad Bessie.

              ROSEY GRIER (CONT'D)
Can we sit down, theirs some things
I want to run by Tookie.

              BAD BESSIE
Yeah, everybody get comfortable.

Rosey sits on the couch, Bad Bessie sits on the couch.
Tookie and Godfather sit in separate chairs.

              ROSEY GRIER
Tookie, I don't know how much you
know about me. I'm an ex-pro
football player. I played eleven
years in the NFL, for the Giants
and Rams.

Tookie appears to be listening.

              ROSEY GRIER (CONT'D)
I run several non-profits and youth
programs. I co-founded American
Neighborhood Enterprises, to help
the disadvantaged buy homes. I've
created a youth program called the
Alpha List.

Tookie's stare turns into a daze, as Rosey's voice ECHOES.

              ROSEY GRIER (CONT'D)
I'm bringing gang leaders in L.A.
together to promote peace. To make
the community better and safer.
The Crips are well known, for all
the wrong things.
              (MORE)

                    ROSEY GRIER (CONT'D)
          I'm hoping you'll help change that.
          As a leader of the Crips, I need
          your help. I'm asking you to join
          the Alpha List. The young cats
          look up to you. If you promote
          peace, they'll follow you.

                    BAD BESSIE
          Tookie! You listening.

Tookie snaps out of his daze.

                    TOOKIE
          Yeah, yeah, I hear you, Mr. Grier.
          I need to think about it.

                    ROSEY GRIER
          Sure. We need to break this cycle
          of gang violence brotha.

Rosey stands up from the couch.

                    ROSEY GRIER (CONT'D)
          Thanks, Bessie, for inviting me.

                    BAD BESSIE
          You're welcome.

Rosey exits out the front door.

                    BAD BESSIE (CONT'D)
               (to Tookie)
          I know what you gon' say.

                    TOOKIE
          I'm not fucken' wit'em. He wants
          to stop gang bangin'. I want to
          keep it goin'. It's Crip or Die
          with me.

EXT. CENTINELA PARK - DAY

A huge contingent of Crips is hanging out on a grass area.
Tookie and Godfather stroll towards the mass.

                    GODFATHER
          Cuz, Jimel is a joke. A lot a
          dudes can't stand him.

                    TOOKIE
          Jimel is cool, he the homie.

                         GODFATHER
              I want to kill that cat and be done
              with his ass.

Loud angry VOICES are heard a commotion is erupting among
Crip gang members. In the middle is an upset, animated
muscle-bound light-complexion 20-year-old male African
American, this is JIMEL BARNES.

He's arguing with CRAZY ED, a male African American 22. They
are about to come to blows.

                         JIMEL BARNES
              Fuck Hoover nigga. This Avalon
              Gardens Crip.

                         CRAZY ED
              Hoover Crip all day mutha fucka.
              We can get down right now.

Suddenly Raymond Washington gets between Jimel and Crazy Ed,
he separates them.

                         RAYMOND WASHINGTON
              Jimel, hold up, we all Crips man.

                         JIMEL BARNES
              Nah, Fuck that Raymond. I'm ah
              knock his ass out.

                         RAYMOND
              Crazy Ed, you wanna go head up with
              Jimel?

                         CRAZY ED
              I'm ready to get down for mine.

Raymond steps aside. Crazy Ed and Jimel square up, Crazy Ed
throws some jabs, and a right left ineffective combination.
Jimel faints with his left, Crazy Ed makes the mistake of
getting too close.

Jimel grabs Crazy Ed, and the tables quickly turn. Crazy Ed
is now on the ground, his legs stretched out. Jimel is now
kneeling behind Crazy Ed and has him in a chokehold.

Everyone is standing around in a trance while an infuriated
Jimel is trying to choke out Crazy Ed. Tookie steps into the
fray, he grabs Jimel, while struggling to restrain Jimel...

                         TOOKIE
              Raymond, grab Crazy Ed.

Raymond pulls Crazy Ed from the grasp of Jimel.

                    JIMEL BARNES
          Let me go Tookie.

Crazy Ed gasped for air as he pulled away from Raymond.

                    CRAZY ED
          You ah dead nigga Jimel.

Several HOOVER CRIPS draw guns on Jimel.

                    TOOKIE
          Aye, man. Be cool now.

Jimel looks uncertain.

                    RAYMOND
          C'mon Crazy Ed, tell yo homeboys to
          put the guns away.

                    CRAZY ED
          This ain't over Jimel -- C'mon,
          let's bail up.

The Hoover Crips lower their guns, but, they're ready to
blast at a moment's notice. Crazy Ed huffs off, the Hoover
Crips follow guns at the ready.

Jimel composes himself, looks at Tookie, he walks off.
Tookie walks over to Raymond.

                    TOOKIE
          I heard you was out of town.

                    RAYMOND
          I was in Texas. I been back for a
          few weeks.

As Crips mill about Bennie Ray Bulldog Simpson walks up.

                    BULLDOG
          Jimel was lucky he didn't get
          killed.

                    TOOKIE
          Raymond, Bulldog help start the
          Hoover Crips.

                    RAYMOND
          You down with them dudes? The
          Hoovers?

                    BULLDOG
          Yeah, shit changed while you was
          locked up.
                    (MORE)

                    BULLDOG (CONT'D)
New sets done started on the east
side, west side, and Compton. It's
a new day Raymond, you better get
with it.

                    RAYMOND
Yeah.

                    BULLDOG
You see what set Jimel claim,
wasn't no Avalon Gardens Crip when
you went to prison.

INT. FREMONT HIGH SCHOOL - HALLWAY - DAY

BIRDIE, a female African American 17, is with TAMMY, a female
African American 17. Their mood is upbeat as they casually
stroll. Suddenly Tammy stops, and the mood quickly changes.

                    BIRDIE
What's wrong?

A group of CRIPLETTES, led by DEBBIE, a female African
American 17, walks up to Tammy. Birdie looks perplexed.

                    DEBBIE
Tammy, you about to get yo ass
kicked.

                    TAMMY
Debbie, You ain't kickin' nobody's
ass.

                    DEBBIE
Bitch, my man is off-limits.

                    TAMMY
The nigga don't want you no more,
so you want to blame me. Bitch you
trippin'.

Debbie draws her fist back, Tammy prepares to defend herself.
The Criplettes are ready to jump in. With aggression, Birdie
steps in front of Tammy.

                    BIRDIE
Y'all ain't fixin' to jump on my
friend. That ain't goin' down.

                    DEBBIE
Bitch, you can get jumped too.

                    BIRDIE
          Cuz you a Criplette, that shit
          don't scare me. If I get jumped,
          you got problems. My cousin
          Raymond Washington will have you
          fucked up.

Debbie pauses.

                    DEBBIE
          Raymond ain't yo cousin.

                    BIRDIE
          Jump on us and you gon' find out.

Just then a campus SECURITY GUARD intervenes.

                    SECURITY GUARD
          OK, girls, let's get to class.

Debbie pointing.

                    DEBBIE
          You better not be lying.

Debbie, with the Criplettes, walks off.

INT. GRANDMOTHER HOUSE - LIVING ROOM - DAY

The TV is on, Violet sits on the couch PHONE RECEIVER to her
ear. She is talking to Raymond.

                    VIOLET
          I'm fine.

                    RAYMOND (V.O.)
          How's grandma?

                    VIOLET
          She's doing well.

                    RAYMOND (V.O.)
          Good. I got promoted to supervisor
          at my job.

                    VIOLET
          Really! That's great Raymond.

INT. RAYMOND WASHINGTON'S APARTMENT - LIVING ROOM - DAY

Moving boxes lay around. PHONE in his hand, RECEIVER to his ear, Raymond attempts to organize things whilst talking to Violet.

                    RAYMOND
          I have more good news. I have my
          own place, ah one bedroom.

                    VIOLET (V.O.)
          Oh, Raymond, I'm so proud of you.

                    RAYMOND
          Thanks, ma.

                    VIOLET (V.O.)
          You're staying away from gangs,
          right?

                    RAYMOND
          C'mon ma, I'm not goin' backward.

                    VIOLET (V.O.)
          Gangs ain't nothing but trouble
          Son. Keep taking care of business,
          you hear me?

                    RAYMOND
          I will ma. I just wanted to hear
          your voice. I'll call you soon,
          ok.

                    VIOLET (V.O.)
          Alright baby, bye.

                    RAYMOND
          Bye,ma.

Raymond hangs up the phone, there is a KNOCK at the door.

I/E. RAYMOND WASHINGTON'S APARTMENT - CONTINUOUS

Raymond opens the door, and staring at him through the SCREEN DOOR is Debbie.

                    RAYMOND
          Yeah.

                    DEBBIE
          I'm looking for Raymond Washington.

             RAYMOND
Who are you?

             DEBBIE
Debbie from Kitchen Crip.

             RAYMOND
What you want?

             DEBBIE
You got ah cousin name Birdie?

Raymond opens the Screen Door, he steps out onto the upstairs
balcony. With a stern look, he stands before Debbie.

             DEBBIE (CONT'D)
I got a problem with her homegirl
Tammy. Now Birdie wants to get
involved, she threw yo name in the
mix, talkin' bout you gon' get me
fucked up if I have her jumped on.
I'm gon' fuck Tammy up, Birdie
needs to mind her business.

             RAYMOND
How'd you find me?

             DEBBIE
I asked some of the homeboys.

             RAYMOND
Birdie is my cousin, I don't know
Tammy. All I have to say about the
matter is, don't fuck with Birdie,
simple as that.

Debbie looks undaunted.

EXT. BIRDIE'S HOUSE - RESIDENTIAL STREET - DAY

Four LOWRIDERS hit the block, each Lowrider is loaded with
black youths. They come to a stop, one Lowrider, in
particular, blows its HORN several times.

The car door opens and out steps Debbie. She walks to the
middle of a walkway, and stands, looking at the window.

The CURTAIN on the window pulls back, Birdie looks out. She
can see Debbie standing in the middle of the walkway. The
curtain closes, and within seconds the FRONT DOOR opens.
Birdie steps out on the front porch.

                         BIRDIE
          What you want?

                         DEBBIE
          I talked to Raymond.

                         BIRDIE
          And?

                         DEBBIE
          He said you his cousin. I told him
          I'm gon' fuck yo friend up. He
          said he don't know Tammy, but leave
          you alone.

                         BIRDIE
          I'm ah stay down with Tammy, ain't
          nothing gon' change about that.

                         DEBBIE
          You get a pass. But I'm gon' catch
          Tammy, believe that.

Debbie gets back in the Lowrider, the caravan drives off.

EXT. INGLEWOOD APARTMENT BUILDING - NIGHT

INSERT CARD: COOLIE COOLS 1979

Looking like a Hawaiian resort, complete with tiki totem
poles, and torches on either side of a plank bridge that
leads to a glass double-door entrance.

INT. INGLEWOOD APARTMENT BUILDING - COURTYARD - NIGHT

A black PCP DEALER is making a transaction. ADDICT #1 and
ADDICT #2, both black, are buying...

                         ADDICT #1
          Give me two sherm sticks.

                         ADDICT #2
          Give me one.

Both Addict #1 and Addict #2 pull out their money. The PCP
Dealer pulls out a large Plastic Zip Bag that contains
SHERMAN CIGARETTES, he takes three from the bag.

                         PCP DEALER
                   (smiling)
          Three freshly dipped wet daddies.

Tookie and WAYNE, a male African American 22, walk through the glass double doors. They observe the buy that's going down.

Money and dope are exchanged, and the buy is completed. Addict #1 and Addict #2 walk off, and the PCP Dealer looks satisfied.

                    TOOKIE
               (to Wayne)
          That's the dude.

Tookie and Wayne walk directly up to the PCP Dealer.

                    WAYNE
          Aye man, I wanna get some sherm.

                    PCP DEALER
          Ten dollars ah stick.

Wayne pulls out a twenty-dollar bill. The PCP Dealer reaches into his coat and pulls out the Plastic Zip Bag containing Sherman Cigarettes. BAM! Tookie punches the PCP Dealer, he's dazed and falls to the pavement.

Tookie goes through the PCP Dealer's pockets, taking a wad of cash. Wayne picks up the Plastic Zip Bag containing the Sherman Cigarettes that are laying on the ground.

                    TOOKIE
          Let's go.

Tookie and Wayne casually stroll off. The PCP Dealer, groggy from the punch, manages to retrieve a 25-caliber pistol that's strapped to his ankle.

He points, pulls the trigger, the gun misfires, CLICK. Tookie stops in his tracks and turns around. The PCP Dealer is still on the pavement holding the gun.

In vain he pulls the trigger, no luck. Tookie and Wayne rush up to the PCP Dealer, giving him the beating of his life.

EXT. RESIDENTIAL STREET - NIGHT

A 1968 CHEVY NOVA parks next to a curb.

INT. 1968 CHEVY NOVA - NIGHT

Wayne is behind the wheel, and Tookie, sitting in the front passenger seat, digs in his pocket. He pulls out a wad of cash, counting it. Tookie looks at Wayne.

                         TOOKIE
              Wayne, there is almost two thousand
              dollars here.

Tookie gives Wayne some money, he counts it. Tookie puts the
rest of the cash in his pocket.

                         WAYNE
              This is only six hundred dollars.
              Shouldn't I get half?

                         TOOKIE
              Nah. Let me see the sherm sticks.

Wayne reaches under the front seat. He grabs the Plastic Zip
Bag containing Sherman Cigarettes, he gives it to Tookie.

                         WAYNE
              What you gon' do with it?

Tookie opens the Plastic Zip Bag, gets a Sherman Cigarette,
and puts it in his mouth.

                         TOOKIE
              Smoke this shit.

Tookie lights the Sherman Cigarette and takes a long drag, he
blows the smoke from his mouth. Tookie looks at Wayne.

                         TOOKIE (CONT'D)
              You wanna hit it.

                         WAYNE
              Nah, I'm cool.
                   (frowning waving his hand
                    in front of his face)
              That shit has a strong smell.

Wayne rolls down the car window. Tookie takes another drag
from the Sherman Cigarette.

                         WAYNE (CONT'D)
              You talk to your mother?

                         TOOKIE
              Not since she kicked me out of the
              house. Your dad, Fred, we got
              along ok. I think he left mama cuz
              of me.

                         WAYNE
              I don't think so. Some people just
              grow apart.

                    TOOKIE
          Maybe.

                    WAYNE
          -- What if that dude's gun hadn't
          jammed?

                    TOOKIE
          Maybe we woulda got shot.

                    WAYNE
          Tookie, If you had to choose
          between death row or life in
          prison. What would you choose?

Tookie nonchalantly takes a drag from the Sherman Cigarette
and blows out the smoke.

                    TOOKIE
          Death row.

                    WAYNE
          Death Row. Why?

                    TOOKIE
          We already livin' on death row,
          bidin' our time. There's no
          difference to me.

INT. RAYMOND WASHINGTON'S APARTMENT - LIVING ROOM - DAY

Raymond Washington has a 45 RECORD in his hand. He places it
on the TURNTABLE.

MUSIC CUE: "Ain't No Stoppin' Us Now " by McFadden &
Whitehead

Raymond vibes to the music. Ray Rhone is sitting on the
couch. Raymond walks over to Ray Rhone, they give each other
FIVE.

                    RAY RHONE
          Man, Raymond, you got a tight crib.

                    RAYMOND
          It's good to see you, Ray. It's
          been a while.

                    RAY RHONE
          I had to come check you out -- Aye
          man, you been keeping up with
          what's happenin' with the Crips?

                    RAYMOND
               (frowns)
          Man, them dudes are out of control.
          I can't keep up. All the different
          Crip sets popping up everywhere.

END MUSIC CUE:

                    RAY RHONE
          I bet you never thought it would
          turn out that way.

                    RAYMOND
          I just wanted to be like the Black
          Panthers. Create unity among
          blacks, an organization that could
          help the Community.

                    RAY RHONE
          I can dig it, man. You had good
          intentions brotha.

                    RAYMOND
          The shit was fucked up from the
          start. I was part of the problem.
          It's a different generation now. I
          started something that has become a
          plague, ah monster.

INT. JACKIE'S POOL HALL - NIGHT

A few people are shooting pool. Standing next to the bar,
Tookie, animated, lashes out at JACKIE, a male African
American 30.

                    JACKIE
          Calm down Tookie.

                    TOOKIE
          Jackie, cuz, don't nobody pull ah a
          gun on me like that.

                    JACKIE
          Pee Pee was looped on sherm man!

FLASHBACK:

INT. BODY SHOP - DAY

Everything is moving in slow motion. PEE PEE, a male African American 23, pushes a young black WOMAN to the side. He points a 45-caliber PISTOL at Tookie, who doesn't blink.

>   PEE PEE
>   (voice distorted)
>   Tookie don't tell me how to treat
>   my woman.

Jackie, mouthing, gestures for Pee Pee to put the gun down. CAPONE, a male African American 23, runs out of the back door. EMPLOYEES working on cars, scurry around seeking safety.

END OF FLASHBACK:

INT. JACKIE'S POOL HALL - NIGHT

Tookie is upset and agitated, and Jackie looks dejected.

>   JACKIE
>   When a person is on PCP, they don't
>   know what they're doing. Just let
>   that shit slide man.

Tookie walks towards the exit.

>   JACKIE (CONT'D)
>   Don't do nothing stupid Tookie.

Tookie walks through the exit door, it slowly shuts behind him.

EXT. JACKIE'S POOL HALL - CONTINUOUS

Standing on the sidewalk just below the Marquee is Tookie. He lights up a Sherman Cigarette and hits it like a joint.

Capone drives up, he jumps out of his CAR with a double-barreled SHOTGUN.

>   CAPONE
>   (excited)
>   Where he at cuz? I'm ready.

Jackie comes out the front door entrance, he sees Capone with the Shotgun. Shocked, Jackie's eyes are wide open. Tookie calmly hits the Sherman Cigarette. He shakes Jackie's hand.

TOOKIE
I'll be back later. Capone, let's
go.

INT. CAPONE'S CAR - NIGHT

High, sitting in the passenger seat, deafly quiet, Tookie
hits the Sherman Cigarette. He passes it to Capone, who is
driving with one hand on the steering wheel, and takes the
Sherman Cigarette with the other hand. Capone takes a long
drag from the Sherman Cigarette and passes it back to Tookie.
Suddenly, the interior illuminates RED.

EXT. WATTS - CENTRAL AVENUE - CONTINUOUS

Red LIGHTS flash from the roof of a SHERIFF POLICE CAR.
Capone's car pulls over to the curb. Over the MEGAPHONE
SHERIFF OFFICER #1 blares out...

SHERIFF OFFICER #1
Driver, passenger, exit the car
with both hands raised.

Another Sheriff Police Car pulls up fast, both car doors fly
open. Two Sheriff's Officers emerge, guns drawn at Capone.

Capone steps out, arms raised. Tookie steps out arms raised.
Four Sheriff Officers with guns pointed at Capone and Tookie
cautiously approach.

Capone and Tookie are now handcuffed, and sitting on the
curb. Two Sheriff Officers are searching through Capone's
car.

One of the Sheriff's Officers takes the key out of the
ignition. He walks to the back of Capone's car and opens the
trunk. Laying there is a double-barreled SHOTGUN.

I/E. SHERIFF STATION - JAIL HALLWAY - CELL - NIGHT

Tookie, isolated by himself, sits on his bunk.

A door opens, and two Sheriff Officers are dragging Capone.

Tookie gets up from his bunk, he peers out the small opening
of his cell door.

CAPONE
I don't wanna go to jail. I ain't
did nothing, man. I wanna go home.

Tookie looks on as Capone is dragged past his cell kicking. One Sheriff Officer opens a cell door, the other Sheriff Officer struggles to get Capone in the cell.

Capone, now in a chokehold by the Sheriff Officer, is viciously punched several times in the gut by the other Sheriff Officer. Both Sheriff Officers toss Capone into the cell, slamming the door shut.

> CAPONE (CONT'D)
> (crying screaming)
> Let me outta here. Please let me
> outta here.

Tookie still peering out the small opening of his cell door.

> TOOKIE
> (shouts)
> Capone -- Capone -- Capone.

Moments later, the same two Sheriff Officers return. They are with Sheriff Officer #1 pounding a NIGHTSTICK in his hand. They walk into Capone's cell, the door is shut behind them.

Tookie, with an uncertain look, listens.

> SHERIFF OFFICER #1 (O.C.)
> (yelling)
> Did that nigger do it?

INT. SHERIFF'S STATION - CAPONE'S CELL - NIGHT

Standing, fear is all over Capone's face. The two Sheriff Officers, Sheriff Officer #1 holding the Nightstick, look extremely intimidating.

> SHERIFF OFFICER #1
> Did he murder those people? Or was
> it you nigger?

> CAPONE
> (wails)
> I don't know nothing about a
> murder. I ain't murder nobody.

The two Sheriff Officers grab hold of Capone, and he struggles. Sheriff Officer #1 shoves the Nightstick in Capone's gut. He collapses to the floor.

The two Sheriff Officers unleash swift kicks to Capone's body, and he shrieks in agony. Sheriff Officer #1 commences hammering Capone's body with the Nightstick.

                    SHERIFF OFFICER #1
            Who did it, who did it, who did it?

FLASHBACK:

INT. CONVENIENCE STORE - MORNING

Tookie burst in wielding a 12 GAUGE SAWED-OFF SHOTGUN. Three
vague male BLACKS rob the TILL. Tookie jams his weapon into
the back of 26-year-old, white male store clerk ALBERT OWENS.
With the muzzle of the shotgun, Tookie forces Owens to walk
to the stockroom.

INT. CONVENIENCE STORE - STOCKROOM - CONTINUOUS

The 12 Gauge Sawed-Off Shotgun is pointed at Owens, his back
is to Tookie and his hands are up in the air.

                    TOOKIE
            Lay down, got damn it.

Owens lays flat on his stomach. Tookie fires two shots into
his back. Boom! Boom!

I/E. SOUTH L.A. MOTEL - ROOM - NIGHT

INSERT CARD: TWO WEEKS LATER

Extremely loud BANGING wakes ROBERT YANG, male Asian 40, from
his sleep. Yang then hears GUN BLASTS and SCREAMING. Yang
leaps from his bed and races out the door.

INT. SOUTH L.A. MOTEL - OFFICE - CONTINUOUS

Yang rushes inside he finds a horrifying sight. His 63-year-
old mother, TSAI-SHAI YANG, Asian, his father YEN-I YANG, 76,
Asian, and his sister YEE-CHEN LIN, 43, Asian. All dying
from shotgun wounds.

END OF FLASHBACK:

INT. SHERIFF STATION - CAPONE'S CELL - NIGHT

The two Sheriff Officers stand over Capone. Sheriff Officer
#1 Nightstick cocked back ready to strike. Capone SCREAMS!

                    CAPONE
          Yes, yes, yes, he did it. He did
          it, I'll say whatever you want.
          Please stop beating me.

EXT. SOUTH LOS ANGELES - SAN PEDRO STREET - DAY

Raymond Washington, gangsta lean stride, casually strolls
sipping on an RC COLA. A CAR slowly pulls up on the side of
Raymond. Behind the wheel is JAMES WARD, a male African
American 22.

                    JAMES WARD
          Raymond!

Raymond turns around -- a smile dawns on his face.

                    RAYMOND
          James Ward, what's up young buck?

Raymond walks up to the car.

                    JAMES WARD
          When did you get back in town?

                    RAYMOND
          I've been back for a while.

                    JAMES WARD
          What you doing out here by
          yourself? You should have somebody
          with you.

                    RAYMOND
          I'm not worried about nothin' man,
          I'm cool.

                    JAMES WARD
          You staying out of trouble?

                    RAYMOND
          C'mon cuz, you sound like my mama.

                    JAMES WARD
             (smiling)
          I remember when you...

FLASHBACK:

EXT. RESIDENTIAL STREET - JAMES WARD HOUSE - EVENING

A slightly younger James Ward is standing on the porch with
his MOTHER. Across the street, two doors down. They see
Police cars in front of Violet Samuel's HOUSE.

She is standing on her porch talking with LAPD Officers Beno
Hernandez and Robert Michael. Directly across the street
Ward and his Mother can see Raymond Washington peering out
from the side of a neighbor's house.

Ward frantically waves his hands in the air, he gets
Raymond's attention. Ward waves Raymond over, and Raymond
manages to safely make it to Ward's porch. Ward and his
Mother hustle Raymond inside their house.

END OF FLASHBACK:

EXT. SOUTH LOS ANGELES - SAN PEDRO STREET - DAY

Raymond is still standing on the side of James Ward's car,
Ward is sitting behind the wheel. Both are chuckling.

                    RAYMOND
          You and your moms save my ass.

                    JAMES WARD
          We couldn't keep'em from lock'en
          you up though.

                    RAYMOND
          Yeah, you right about that. Hey,
          man, you wanna hang out? I got a
          crib just up the street.

                    JAMES WARD
          I can't, I have to get back home.

                    RAYMOND
          Drop me off at the crib then.

                    JAMES WARD
          Jump in.

Raymond gets in the car, Ward pulls off.

INT. TORRANCE SUPERIOR COURT - DAY

A JUDGE sits behind the bench. Tookie in chains, and wearing
an orange jumpsuit, stands alongside his ATTORNEY.

                         JUDGE
          Mr. Williams, you've been charged
          with four counts of first-degree
          murder, two counts of first-degree
          robbery. How do you plea?

                         TOOKIE
          Not guilty.

A loud GASP is heard from the gallery.

EXT. 6326 S. SAN PEDRO STREET - APARTMENT BUILDING - NIGHT

INSERT CARD: AUGUST 9TH, 1979 10 PM

Downstairs, Raymond Washington is talking to RICKY BENJAMIN,
a male black 30. A FOUR-DOOR SEDAN drives up, and a SHADOWY
FIGURE sitting in the back seat calls out...

                         SHADOWY FIGURE
                    (friendly)
          Aye, Raymond, what's goin' on
          brotha, how you doin'?

                         RAYMOND
                    (to Ricky)
          I know that car right there.

Ricky watches as Raymond walks up to the car. It appears
Raymond is talking to the Shadowy Figure, then BOOM! from a
Shotgun. The Four-Door Sedan speeds off.

Ricky races to Raymond's side as he lays on his back holding
his stomach.

                         RICKY BENJAMIN
          Raymond, damn.

                         RAYMOND
          Ricky, he shot me, man.

                         RICKY BENJAMIN
          Who was it?

                         RAYMOND
          I know that dude. He shot me.

                         RICKY BENJAMIN
          What's the dude's name?

                    RAYMOND
               (weak)
          I'll get the dudes. They gon' pay.

                    RICKY BENJAMIN
          Raymond, hang in there brotha.

INT. LOS ANGELES COUNTY JAIL - DAY

Tookie sits in a booth PHONE to his ear, he looks through a
GLASS PARTITION. On the other side of the booth looking
through the Glass Partition, the phone to her ear is Bad
Bessie.

                    TOOKIE
               (frustrated)
          They railroadin' me. Mutha fucka's
          on the witness stand lying on me.
          Prosecutor making deals with
          snitches to testify against me.

                    BAD BESSIE
          I got more bad news.

                    TOOKIE
          That's the last thing I need.

                    BAD BESSIE
          It's Raymond, he's dead. Somebody
          shot him.

                    TOOKIE
          Ah man, damn -- who did it?

                    BAD BESSIE
          Don't know. I heard he walked up
          to a car, Raymond thought he knew
          the person. The dude shot him.

                    TOOKIE
          That don't make any sense. Raymond
          no better than to walk up to a
          nigga in ah car.

                    BAD BESSIE
          Well, that's what I heard.

INT. TORRANCE SUPERIOR COURT - DAY

INSERT CARD: APRIL 15TH, 1981

The Judge sits behind the bench. Tookie, dressed in a blazer, open collar dress shirt, sits next to his Attorney. The PRESIDING JUROR hands the Judge a jury FORM.

> JUDGE
> I have received the verdict which now will be read -- The defendant will rise and harken to its verdict.

Tookie and his Attorney stand up.

The FOREPERSON with the verdict in hand.

> FOREPERSON
> The State of California versus Stanley Williams, case number 1003. We the jury, duly held and sworn in the above and title cause, do find our verdicts upon the counts submitted to us as follows. Guilty on all four counts of first-degree murder, and two counts of first-degree robbery.

Subtle elation is heard from the FAMILIES seated in the gallery.

Tookie unfazed, stoic look on his face. Tookie's Attorney rubs his shoulders.

> FADE OUT.

OVER CREDITS: PHOTOS OF ACTUAL CRIPS & BLOODS EVOLUTION AND MIGRATION FROM CALIFORNIA THROUGHOUT THE UNITED STATES AND ABROAD.

The End.